Tea with Milk and Murder

Tea with Milk and Murder

A Daisy Fields Cozy Mystery

Katie O'Neil

Copyright © 2025 by Katie O'Neil
ISBN: 9978-1-9192363-1-5

All rights reserved.
No part of this book may be reproduced in any form or by any electronic or mechanical means, including information storage and retrieval systems, without written permission from the author, except for the use of brief quotations in a book review.

The story, all names, characters, and incidents portrayed in this book are fictitious. No identification with actual persons (living or deceased), places, buildings, and products is intended or should be inferred.

For my Family

A Note on Spelling

Before you report any suspicious spellings, let me assure you: they're not typos, they're just written in the British flavour of English, with some Cymraeg (Welsh) thrown in for some extra tasty seasoning. You'll find *neighbours* doing *favours* with that extra vowel, and the occasional *boot* that's actually the trunk of a car. Think of it all as part of the setting: quirky, charming, and just a little mysterious. So please don't fret about any dodgy spellings you don't recognise (instead of recognize) while you analyse (not analyze) the clues and no, you can't arrest the spelling!

Of course, I am but human, if there are any genuine mistakes please get in touch with me at Katie@katieoneilmysteries.com

Chapter One

The sweet Elderflower and Raspberry steam swirled into Daisy's face as she filled the fine china teapot. Turning away, she blew up inside her glasses to clear the fog, instead managing to release a stray curl from its precarious position sat atop the thick red frames and landing straight down over her left eye. With a sigh, she flattened it back over her hair, knowing time was against her before it pinged back down her face again.

She placed the teapot next to the mismatched teacup on the tray, its hand painted raspberry design chosen carefully from her shelf to match the tea. Turning them just so, she made sure each would display their decorated side to the customers as she carried them through to the table.

The sounds of chinking china, children's laughter, and gossip filled the air as Daisy walked back through the beaded curtain into the tea shop. She'd always loved that threshold, from the pristine, modern cleanliness of the kitchen, that was dominated by white walls and cupboards and stainless steel surfaces, into the cluttered warmth of the teashop. From the heavily patterned wallpaper that Aunt Poppy had carefully chosen, to the large Welsh dressers that were filled with delicate china, too old to be used but too precious to throw away, having been donated by various villagers over the years. A random collection of small pedestal tables filled the room, surrounded by an even more random collection of chairs. Everything screamed Victorian decadence.

A pang of nostalgia hit her as she recalled the first time she walked through those doors as a shy four-year-old visiting her aunt alone for the first time. It was like a small girl's dream, a place where everyone had tea parties with fancy china and dainty cakes all served up on lacy tablecloths.

"Here you go Mrs Roberts, you're about to christen my brand new batch, slightly more elderflower this year, so I'm hoping you enjoy it." Mrs Roberts placed her crocheting into her lap and smiled up at her. This was the first face she had met all those years ago, a kind, caring face with the typically short bouffant hair style of the older lady that visits the hair salon every week for a shampoo and set.

Daisy had no idea of her age, but to her, she had always been the elderly lady who might look frail in her calf length dresses, always paired with a coordinating, hand knitted cardigan of course, but was tougher than most men around. If the rumours were anything to be believed, and Daisy did truly believe, Mrs Roberts had even chased down a pickpocket and knocked him out with her handbag on a day trip to Cardiff once.

Daisy had learnt her lesson at the tender age of twelve, when being mortified really sticks with you, about not presuming a woman's age. She had once presumed the bonnie baby bouncing on visitors knee was the woman's grandchild and the woman in question must have been in her sixties if she was a day. It turned out the woman in question was thirty-eight and the baby was indeed hers. To this day, the memory of the woman's offended face still haunted her, and she had never dared verbalise her presumptions since.

"Daisy, you tweak this recipe every year, and every year I

think 'This is it, the perfect blend' and the next year I'm happy to be proven wrong once again." She patted Daisy's arm. "I've changed my mind, though. I was going to be good, but I've decided I will have a little treat after all. No. Surprise me or I'll always choose the toasted teacake to be safe." She added quickly as Daisy attempted to give her a list of today's specials.

Daisy smiled politely, trying hard not to chuckle. They repeated this same charade most weeks. Mrs Roberts had been visiting the tea shop every Thursday since Daisy could remember. She and Aunty Poppy had been the closest of friends for many years. Every week Mrs Roberts would order just a pot of tea and only rarely did she choose a treat, yet every week Poppy would always surprise her with that day's special.

Daisy had never quite had the guts to produce something without a request, feeling that it may disrespect the woman she now classed as a friend, and thus, this charade remained. But this arrangement suited them, and on the odd Thursday when Mrs. Roberts didn't change her mind, Poppy felt torn between partial gratitude for not presuming and partial guilt for not offering something.

"I know just the thing to go with your tea." She threaded her way between the tables and chairs, smiling and waving at patrons as she passed, returning from the kitchen a few moments later with a side plate. "Here you go. It's a set custard tart with raspberry compote and a thyme biscuit base."

"Oh that sounds scrummy, now off you go and get ready for your rush." Mrs Roberts' eyes sparkled as she turned the plate to admire the wobble on the custard, while simultaneously wafting her other hand in Daisy's direction signalling her dismissal.

Behind the counter stood Michael. Original to the shop the counter was showing its age and Daisy made a mental note to get someone in to sand and repaint it.

Michael, with his long dark hair tied back in a neat, hair

netted bun beneath his chef's cap, was Daisy's assistant. He had turned up at the shop one Saturday five years previous, at barely fourteen years old with a plate of perfect chocolate eclairs and wearing a full set of chef's whites, including the cap. He had vowed to work for free and do anything she asked of him if she would just let him help with the baking for practice and work experience so he could one day become a patisserie chef.

Of course Daisy had paid him for every hour he worked and had ensured that everything was above board with both his parents and the law. Now two years through his college course and on the verge of heading to university, his fashion choices had broadened with a whole rainbow of chef coats. Today's was a dark denim.

"Michael, make sure the urn is full and prepare for a rush will you, please? John the Bus asked Mrs Roberts to let us know he'll be bringing a bus full down from the museum soon." Leaning against the counter, she looked out over the tea shop.

The group of toddlers in the children's area all looked to be getting to that fidgety stage. One was already sitting on his mother's lap, rubbing his eyes as another let out a loud yawn. She only needed one of the mothers to decide it was nap time and start getting ready to leave, and the whole group would quickly disperse.

Apart from Mrs Roberts, there were only a few other villagers dotted around. She mentally counted the chairs available before following Michael through to the kitchen. "I think I'll start dishing up portions of jam and clotted cream. You know how these groups love their cream teas. Ah, seems like you read my mind. I guess I'll go and make sure the tables are clean and ready, then." Michael was already pulling the piles of small ramekins down from their shelf, the large silver urn issuing its telltale rattle as it worked towards reaching a boil in the corner.

"Leave this to me, Chef. I'll be done before the first backside hits a floral chair covering." Daisy rolled her eyes at his shoulders, jiggling as he chuckled to himself. He had always insisted on calling her chef, even though she hated it. "It's good to make it habit," he argued each time until she simply gave up protesting. The bell above the shop door chimed, and Daisy stuck her head through the beaded curtain.

"Bye ladies, same time next week! I'll make gingerbread men for the babies and some of the pistachio and chocolate biscotti I know you mammies like." She waved at the small children and smiled at the adorable chorus of "ta tas," and blown kisses.

"Oh Daisy. I'll see you soon, girls. I just need to do something first." Sylvia Wentworth, a young mother with a rosy faced baby dozing in a carrier against her chest, waved at Daisy for attention. "Peter's mother is coming for tea and I need something special. You know what she's like. I was going to make something, but we've been up for three nights straight." The cute button nose scrunched, and the baby let out a single sob as his bottom lip stuck out. "Oh, darling, please stay asleep." Sylvia bobbed up and down, bending her knees and swaying as she hushed and patted the back of the carrier.

"Teething?" Daisy asked, taking in the tired circles under Sylvia's eyes and her paler than usual complexion. Sylvia nodded and ran her fingers through her hair.

"I've even taken to walking up and down the street with him in his pram all hours of the night just to have some peace and quiet!" She said, suppressing a yawn.

"I know the perfect pudding for Mrs Wentworth. Michael made a Tarte Tatin this morning." Daisy pointed to the still uncut tart in the display. "I'll get him to pop it up in a bit with some fresh Chantilly cream, so you're all set. I'll also whip up a batch of Aunty Poppy's teething biscuits, too. I think all the villagers, under the age of forty-five, teethed on those things. Oh, don't worry, pay me next time you're here. I think little

Freddie needs you to get moving before he wakes up again. And of course the teethers are on me." A look of relief swept over Sylvia's face and she stopped digging in her rucksack for her purse.

"Thank you so much. I knew you'd come to my rescue!"

No sooner had Sylvia disappeared past the window than another familiar face walked into view, followed by the chiming of the bell above the door.

"They're here Michael." She stuck her head back through the curtain "What are you doing now?" Michael was mixing a large batch of dough and heating both bakestones.

"I had an amazing idea, and I'm annoyed that neither of us have thought of doing this before." Her blank face must have answered his question.

"Fresh Welsh cakes of course! Don't worry, I'll man in here and flip these bad boys while I go. You mark my words, once they are cooking, their noses will start twitching and they won't be able to resist buying half a dozen for the journey home."

"Come on in ladies and gentlemen, the tea shop is the best place for a snack and a cuppa to wet your whistle before we get the bus back down to the carpark." Mary's voice was loud and clear above the hubbub, and she waved at Daisy while ushering the throng of visitors through the door. Daisy smiled and nodded at each face as they filled the tables. She wondered what Aunty Poppy would say if she could see the tea shop now. Would she believe that her quaint little shop would be full to bursting and that tourists would eventually outnumber the regulars with so many far-reaching accents? She smoothed back her loose curls again, grabbed her notepad and made her way through the room as quickly as she could without rushing the customers, taking orders and offering recommendations.

"This is a good crowd!" She said to Mary as they crossed paths by the till. Michael had been right. The smell of the fresh Welsh cakes was filling the room, and she had already heard whispers about the delicious smell with people wanting to know what it might be from as they wanted some.

"Yes, they are a lively bunch. Most of them are Americans here from a cruise ship. They love a good guided tour, the Americans. You should have heard the gasps when the lights went out down in the pit. One lady even screamed." She inclined her head to a well-dressed woman in her fifties sat with a group of friends. "I swear they have giggled and caused more nuisance than some of the school groups we've had!" The next 30 minutes passed by in a blur of orders and steaming pots of tea, she gracefully accepted the compliments with a smile, and the minor criticisms with grace. Although she almost cracked at the insinuation that her lemon drizzle cake was store bought.

"Ladies and gentlemen." Mary's voice quietened the buzz of gossip as all eyes fell on her "The coach will be heading down the valley to the carpark at 2.30pm. please feel free to explore the village. There are plenty of shops selling local produce, the village pub is just at the top of Commercial Street and if you'd prefer to walk back to the carpark, the map at the back of your guide book shows the trail that leads down the valley along the river. Those of you on the Amelia Dove tour group, please note that your bus will head back to the port at 3pm so you'll need to ensure you leave a minimum of an hour to make the walk back in time."

Michael appeared at that moment carrying a large display plate of still warm Welsh cakes and placed them in pride of place at the centre of the display.

"Oh, and don't forget to purchase your locally made tea blends and fresh Welsh cakes here before you leave. They were cooked on a traditional bake stone while you have been sat here. You can't get much fresher than that, ladies and gentlemen! If you'd like your own bake stone, Dewi at the iron mongers has some beautiful ones in his window just three doors down!" She turned back to Daisy and sighed. It was as if her show persona switched off and she visibly relaxed. "Shall I give you a hand with the dishes?"

"No! Go and sit down for five minutes. In here." Daisy ushered her friend into the kitchen "Michael, make sure she sits in that chair and does nothing until she's had at least two cups of tea and a few of those blueberry macarons." Mary had always amazed Daisy with her never ending energy. It was like she never stopped, always being helpful to everyone she met, but Daisy worried that one day she might just run out of steam permanently.

"Yes, Chef" Her assistant raised a mock salute, his hands full of bubbles from the sink of dishes "prisoner, take your seat!" He ordered, pointing towards the tatty old leather wing-back chair with the ripped cushion in the corner.

"You two spoil me. I'd much rather be helping you. I can go and clear the tables. It sounds like people are starting to leave. Will you at least get out there quick so nobody leaves without looking at things to buy, go wave some Welsh cakes under their noses or something?"

"Be right there!" Daisy called back to three women who were peering into the glass case. "You. Stay!" She directed at Mary who, finally submitting to her fate, slumped back into the chair, kicked off her shoes and put her feet up on the footstool.

Michael's plan had worked. The drawer of the old-fashioned till flew open with a clang every few minutes as her shelves and serving dishes emptied of jars of jams, paper bags of tea blends, and boxes of treats.

"Thank you for coming. Enjoy the rest of your day!" Daisy breathed a sigh of relief. The rush was over and apart from one gentleman in the corner, the shop was empty. "Can I get you another pot of tea, sir? Something to eat" She asked as she cleared the tables around him.

'When did the haberdashers close?' His sharp look took her aback.

"Pardon? Oh, the shop closed about fifteen years ago, I think. It was before I moved here and took over from my aunt. Are you from around here?"

"So when were they knocked together? Poppy's place and the haberdashers?" He asked, ignoring her question.

"That was about five years ago. When the pit museum opened and the community council had their plan to regenerate the area. You knew my aunt?" Daisy tried to get a good look at him to see if she recognised him. His once dark hair was now more salt than pepper and although he was probably only in his sixties, he looked old beyond his years, like the world had been unkind to him. But as aged and haggard as his face looked, with deep creases and heavy bags below his eyes, his clothes were immaculate. A dark grey suit, perfectly tailored to him, accented with a bottle green tie and matching silk pocket square, would make him fit right in at a private London gentlemen's club.

"I can't see how that was allowed to happen. Why was the shop empty, anyway? It was a good family business." He said, rapping his fingers on the table as he got more and more agitated.

"I'm sorry, sir, I couldn't tell you. The shop was empty for years. It was on the verge of being redeveloped into flats before Aunty Poppy took it over."

"I'll not bother with another pot." The chair scraped across the wooden floor as he grabbed his duffel coat, stood to his feet, and strode out of the door with a clatter.

What a strange man. Daisy thought to herself as he stormed across the road and up the narrow footpath between the shops that lead to the streets above.

Chapter Two

Daisy sat with a start, her heart racing as she blinked into the darkness. She squinted closely at the illuminated clock face, staring at the blur for half a minute too long not to feel stupid before holding her glasses in front of her eyes. She groaned and lay back down with a thud against her pillow. She never woke before her alarm, thinking that 5am was already an ungodly hour that shouldn't exist in the world, yet it was only just gone 3am.

Expecting to slip straight back onto the white sandy beach with the warm ocean lapping at her feet, she pulled the covers around her and tried to relax. But the sun, sea and sand of her dreams eluded her. She tossed and turned, trying to find a more comfortable spot. With a sigh, she thumped at the pillows, shaping them back into soft, fluffy mounds, kicked at the duvet so it lay flat over her, and squeezed her eyes shut, desperate to steal any moments of extra sleep she could manage.

But instead of sleeping, she soon found herself staring up at the wavy shadows on the artexed ceiling from the light creeping through the gap in her curtains.

Why had she woken up? Had there been a noise?

An owl hooted in the distance, but the night outside her window was still. The nights here were always peaceful now. Not like when she used to fall asleep to the thrumming rumble of the mines when she was a child.

Did she try to catch another hour of sleep? Well, hour and 47 minutes at the current count, or did she admit defeat and start her day now? The list of all the things that needed doing before the tea shop opened rattled through her mind. The loaves that needed time to prove. All the different biscuits and cakes that needed baking. The lunchtime order for the writing group's monthly meeting at the library. Maybe she could use the extra time to try out that new bread recipe Michael had brought in and she'd been promising to bake for a fortnight.

Where was that recipe now, anyway?

"Who am I kidding?" She said aloud to the empty room and pulled herself out from under the warm covers. She squinted at the brightness of the bedside lamp and threw open her wardrobe doors.

By 3:30am she had wrangled her frizzy mass of red curls into a bun, and stood in her small kitchen, dressed in her loose cotton chef trousers and white t-shirt, wrapped in an old shawl of Aunty Poppy's. She absentmindedly stared out of the window, waiting for the kettle to boil as she buttered her toast. A thin crown of amber dawn peeked over the mountain tops, revealing the silhouettes of trees and the big house that stood proudly surveying the valley. The dark, inky sky slowly transforming into a blush of light.

A movement caught her eye, and she peered out through her own reflection, trying to see what it had been. But the darkness in the lane below stopped her from seeing anything beyond herself and the kitchen behind her. On tippy toes, she leaned closer to block out the light.

What was out there?

The dark figure pounced straight at her.

"Argh" Daisy let out a high-pitched scream. Throwing her hands up to protect her face, she jumped back, knocking against the small kitchen table. The knife clattered to the tiled floor, sending splatters of blueberry preserve up the pristine white cupboards, and she waited. Waited for the smashing of glass, for someone to grab her. For something terrible to happen.

But there was nothing.

Her heart beating hard enough to hurt her eardrums, she dared to peek through her fingers. Her eyes falling on the disgruntled and shabby face staring back at her through the glass.

"Barnaby!" She dropped her hands to her side and let out a long sigh of relief then remembered that she lived in a first-floor flat and unless someone was balancing on a ladder or the wall of the steps, there was no way they could pounce into her window like that. Plus, do burglars make a habit of jumping through windows to get into houses, anyway?

The large ginger cat pawed at the window and tilted his head to the side, wondering what all the commotion was about. He disappeared from view before reappearing at the cat flap, his mass of hair pinging back into shape as he squeezed through the small square hole. He stared down at a blob of jam near his feet, sniffed at it, then meowed disapprovingly and sauntered off to his bed.

"You don't actually live here, you know! I can evict you as quickly as I let you in," Daisy called after him as his swishing tail disappeared around the door frame.

Barnaby had appeared on her doorstep two years earlier, a mangy, flea ridden stray, who looked very sorry for himself, and very annoyed with the rest of the world. She'd fed him and left a bowl of fresh water for him at the bottom of her steps, but had shooed him away each time he'd tried to sneak in through the open back door.

None of the regulars recognised the photograph she had pinned to the board in the teashop. Day after day, he returned. She was adamant not to be taken in by his grumpy orange eyes, the rubbing of his squashed face, typical of the Persian breed, along her legs, or his purr, which got increasingly louder when she stopped to stroke him.

She'd given him flea and worming treatment when it became clear he was a stray. Then one fateful December night, as the snow fell, she couldn't bear the sight of him huddled in the corner of her windowsill any longer.

"Okay cat, one night. You don't go any further than the kitchen do you hear me?" She had told him sternly as he'd cautiously wandered inside, watching her incase she changed her mind, then jumped up onto a dining chair falling instantly to sleep. She had kept the heating on that night wanting him to be as warm and comfortable as possible if he was only going to be staying the one night.

Then she had decided he should stay until the snow thawed. He was then allowed to stay until the cold snap was over. Then, when spring brought some drier weather. But by then the cute little cat bowls with the matching fishy mat had appeared on the kitchen floor. One comfy bed sat next to the fire and another, a hammock, hung from the radiator in her bedroom.

She'd spent one afternoon chopping all the mats from his messy fur, discovering in the process that he was just a scrawny, gentle little mite under the angry ball of fluff and that she'd fallen in love with having him around the flat.

Even though she grumbled and swore under her breath at him while she mopped up her breakfast, they both knew there was no way she'd ever actually throw him out.

The morning air was brisk as Daisy stepped out of her back door and hopped down the thirteen steps to the kitchen. The adrenaline still pumped through her veins and she wanted to use it up on some bread dough.

It was like muscle memory. Daisy hummed along to the pop song on the radio as she fell into the familiar routine of switching on all the ovens and wandered the perimeter of the room, taking down the basic ingredients she needed and placed them in their spots. Bread flour, yeast, salt and sugar for the bread against the back wall. Self raising flour, butter, eggs and sugar for the cakes on the side wall, the front wall being home to all the cups and teapots. The island in the centre of the pristine kitchen, filled with shining stainless steel appliances, was where all the biscuits were mixed, rolled, and baked. She placed the large tubs of plain flour and sugar, along with the butter, next to the large mixer.

Nodding in time to the music, she flicked through Aunty Poppy's recipe cards, trying to decide what she felt like making that day, laying each one by their relevant spots and pulled out the additional ingredients.

The new bread recipe!

"Where did Mrs Puw put that piece of paper?" She wondered aloud to herself as she ran through in her mind where she'd last seen it. Michael had brought it in on Saturday, the day after his college day. Mrs Puw had judged the bread for being "altogether too green". The dough containing basil and spinach along with some cheeses. In her mind's eye she watched as the older lady placed the slip of paper down next to the till and Michael rolled his eyes towards her knowing that as much as Mrs Puw hated change, she would always judge a recipe fairly and would highly likely be a fan of "the green bread" given time.

She stepped through the darkness of the shop, running her finger along the edge of the large sideboard that housed the till to her left, and flicked on the ornate lamp in the corner. There, half hidden under the large old-fashioned till, was

Michael's neatly written recipe. She scanned the list, checking she had everything in stock.

Fresh spinach, yup.

Feta cheese...there's a new packet in my fridge upstairs. As she ran through the list in her mind, something caught her eye.

Where the kitchen was clean and minimalist, the tea shop, in comparison, was dark, heavily patterned and overly stuffed, with far too many objects for the space. In the dark of night, everything from the large heavy furniture against the heavily patterned pink walls, to the small round tables and mismatched chairs, spread their shadows in crisscrosses around the room from the lamplight behind her and the brighter streetlight outside the door.

But there was another shadow. A dark mass in the doorway.

Weaving between the tables, the swishing of heavy brocade tablecloths brushing against her legs and her footsteps padding across the wooden floor were deafening in the silence.

Had someone left a bin bag against her door, mistaking her for the charity shop? The dark shape looked large and lumpy through the frosted glass. Peering through the clear lines that swirled and patterned the words Tea Shop in the glass, it looked more like a pile of clothes than a bin bag.

How lazy can people be to not even bother putting their donations in a black bag?

The bolts scraped and scratched as she pulled them back. Turning the handle, she shouted with surprise as the door swung open heavily, pushing her aside and knocking her glasses from her face. The pile of clothes fell with a thud and, as she grappled to catch her glasses and get them safely back on her face, something shiny and gold clattered to the floor and rolled away across the room. Forgotten instantly as Daisy struggled to comprehend the sight at her feet. The pile of clothes that had fallen to the floor wasn't a pile of clothes after all.

The outstretched arm.

The face half hidden by a hat.

Why had this man been sleeping in her doorway?

Why hadn't he moved just as shocked at the door opening behind him as she was with it coming towards her?

A terrible feeling grew in the pit of her stomach.

"Hello, are you okay? What happened?" She said, falling to her knees. The door swung open more, and the hand that had been covering his chest slipped to his side, revealing the blood-stained shirt.

"Oh, my God." she said, her voice barely above a whisper.

With a shaking hand, she lifted the hat away from his eyes. Unblinking eyes that stared at the ceiling without seeing it, eyes that would never see again.

Licking at her parched lips, and with a sinking heart, she felt for a pulse. She knew that there wouldn't be one, yet Daisy still pulled her hand away as quickly as if she'd been burnt. She rubbed her hands together, as if death was contagious and she needed to get rid of it.

There was a dead man in her shop.

What did you do when there was a dead body?

Should she shout for someone?

And then sense sank in. Her body shook and the small amount of breakfast she had managed to eat, threatened to make another appearance as she ran to the phone and dialled 999.

Chapter Three

DI Locke's voice barking orders at the uniformed officers had preceded him up the steps to Daisy's kitchen. She had decided before even setting eyes on him that he was an unpleasant and bossy person. The deep furrows above his heavily circled eyes, the arms folded tightly across his chest, and the repetitive tapping of his right foot on the tiled floor also told her that he was not a morning person.

"Now Miss Fields. You didn't hear or see anything in the street before you opened the door?"

"Inspector Locke. Daisy has already been through all of this with Tom, as well as one of your own officers. I don't think it's a good idea to make her relive it all again." Said Mrs Puw, who stood protectively over Daisy, her hair still in curlers. She had arrived just a few moments after the police cars and, after forcing her way through the crowd, had dared any officer to stop her from getting up the steps into the flat.

The remains of a cup of extra sweet tea still in her hands, Daisy was grateful to her friend and employee for coming to her rescue. Mrs Puw had been her aunt's friend and confidant for many years. She had watched over Daisy as she grew, never afraid to reprimand her when she was a naughty little girl or admonish her poor choices as an awkward teen and yet celebrated every piece of good news and every milestone, even when she was at home with her parents. Now, just as she had done when Aunty Poppy was nearing the end, she was watching over and protecting her.

Daisy wasn't new to dead bodies. Her previous life as a victim support worker had seen her in many terrible situations.

But not here.

Not in her little tea shop in the heart of this tight knit community.

This was supposed to be her safe space.

"It's vitally important I get all this information. Some relevant questions may have been missed earlier, or Miss Fields may recall something now that she had previously forgotten or not deemed important to share." Inspector Locke's lips pursed, and he puffed out his chest as if shocked at being questioned by an elderly member of the public.

"It's okay Mrs Puw. I don't mind answering the Inspector's questions." Daisy pulled her cardigan tighter around her body. Mrs Puw frowned, Daisy thought she might actually argue her case. But she simply sighed and busied herself filling the kettle again while muttering under her breath.

"Not that I can tell you anything different to what I told Tom. I mean Sergeant Griffith." Daisy said to the Inspector. It wasn't often that outside police came into the valley and Daisy didn't want Tom to get into trouble for anything she said or did, like talking about him on overly friendly terms.

"Now Miss Fields. I would be very grateful if you could go through everything that happened this morning. Right from the very beginning. Milk, two sugars." He directed the last sentence to Mrs Puw before dragging a chair out from under the table. The screeching noise as it scraped across the tile sending Barnaby hissing back out through the flap where he had just stuck his nose in to investigate.

With a dull ache beginning to grow behind her eyes, Daisy recounted everything from the moment she woke up to the moment she called the police whilst simultaneously wondering whether the Inspector had noticed how heavy-handed Mrs Puw had become with the teapot and cups behind her.

"And you don't remember any noise after you woke up?" They had been going round in circles for the last half an hour. DI Locke asking the same questions over and over but from a slightly different angle or with minor tweaks in the wording. Had she heard anything, seen anything? Had anything unusual happened over the last few days, weeks?

Daisy pressed two fingers into each temple, rubbing in small, hard circles, trying to dissipate the pain that had grown behind her eyes. She had tried to stay patient, understanding the Inspector had a job, but that patience was now threadbare and at risk of snapping.

"Miss Fields?"

"Please call me Daisy." She said with a deep, cleansing breath.

"Daisy...Fields?" There was that familiar bemused look on his face as he spoke her name slowly.

"Yes, and I've heard it all before. Yes, it's what my parents actually called me. No, I don't know what they were thinking. No, they weren't hippies. Yes, I was teased relentlessly in school, and yes. I have told you everything. I didn't hear anything, I didn't see anything. I woke up early, but I went about my morning, the same as I have done every day since I moved here. I really don't know what else I can tell you." Once she started, she couldn't stop the words tumbling out of her mouth and she felt a little guilty for being short with him. But the inspector either didn't notice her tone or chose to ignore it.

"Yes, and I am grateful. Now I've another few questions for you." The inspector held his tea cup out to Mrs Puw, who hovered around the kitchen, making herself look busy. He nodded at the cup with raised eyebrows, signalling his expectance. She scowled, refilled it, and then banged the milk jug and the sugar bowl down on the table next to him.

Attention back on Daisy, his saccharine smile doing nothing to put her at ease, he pushed on.

"Do you recognise the man that you found?" He asked, stirring the sugars into his tea.

"No, I don't believe so."

"You said yourself it was pretty dark. Maybe you didn't get a good look?"

"No, I said it wasn't very dark. I had the lamp on in the shop and the streetlight is just outside the door. I didn't recognise him." She took a deep breath and asked outright, "Is this questioning going somewhere, Inspector?"

"How long exactly have you been running the teashop downstairs?" He ignored her and continued.

"Since my aunt passed away six years ago. I don't know what this has to do with—"

"And that's why you moved here? To take over the tea shop?" He cut her off.

"No, I moved here to take care of my aunt when she became unwell." An uneasy feeling grew in the pit of her stomach.

"And where did you live before coming here, Miss Fields?"

"In London. Although I don't know what that has to do with any of this."

"Seems like a drastic change of scenery. Coming to this little dead end valley, from the glitzy life of the big city?"

"Not really. I spent a lot of my childhood here. I always loved the valley, and this opportunity seemed like one I couldn't miss. It was what my aunt wanted, after all. She left the shop to me."

"I believe you had some issues forcing you to leave your previous job?" And there it was. He had done his homework.

She tried to form a carefully worded question in her mind to find out how much he could have possibly found out in such a short space of time, but before her poor aching brain could get itself into gear, Mrs Puw had strode over to the back door, swung it open and was gesturing for the inspector to leave.

"Now Inspector Locke. I must insist you let Daisy be for today. She has had a terrible shock, but I'm sure she will be more than happy to answer your questions tomorrow."

"Of course. Where are my manners?" The scraping of the chair across the floor hit every single nerve in Daisy's body. *Why can't you lift it like a normal person?* She wanted to scream at him. "I'll leave you with my card. Please do let me know if you think of anything that could help the investigation." He was shouting orders at the officers below before the door had fully slammed shut behind him.

"Would you believe the cheek of him?" Mrs Puw said over the sound of the water running into the kettle. "To come in here bringing up all that stuff that has nothing to do with that poor, poor dead man downstairs. God rest his soul. What on earth did he think he would achieve?" Mrs Puw's voice drifted into the distance as Daisy's thoughts took over. London hadn't entered her head in a long time. Could the man downstairs really have anything to do with that?

"Hiya Daisy. Mrs Puw. Oh fab. Perfect timing for a cuppa?" Tom Griffith, local police sergeant and Daisy's friend for life after she shared her red crayon with him in the chapel's Sunday School, pulled off his fluorescent jacket and flopped down in the chair Detective Inspector Locke had just vacated. Tall and slim, he never seemed to look comfortable sat at her small table as if he had too much legs to fit underneath.

"Daisy will be going for a nap now, in a minute Tom."

"No, I'm fine Mrs Puw, honest." Daisy said, already feeling much calmer now the inspector's barrage of questions had ended. Although a nap really did sound lovely. "Can you tell us anything, Tom? That Inspector Locke didn't give up any information at all."

"That inspector Locke is a tyrant. He's treating us like imbeciles. Doesn't think we have any idea how to do our jobs at all. Okay, we're not big-city police like he is, but we've all been on the same training! Oh, thanks Mrs Puw. I don't suppose there's anything going to eat, is there? I haven't had any breakfast yet, and the tyrant won't let anyone leave." Mrs Puw fussed his hair and muttered about the state of the world as the frying pan, already sat over the flames, began warming behind her.

"Tom. Forget about your stomach for a minute, will you? What's going on in my shop? Does anyone know who that poor man is?" It came out louder than Daisy had expected and she slunk back in her chair, her fingers pressed to her lips.

"What? Oh yeah, it's John Foster. Gareth the Milk recognised him." Tom said, grabbing the biscuit tin from the sideboard behind him.

"Who's John Foster?" Daisy asked. Trying to scrape at the tiny hint of recollection at the back of her mind.

"I'll tell you who John Foster is." Mrs Puw said, throwing bacon haphazardly into the sizzling pan. "He is the scum of the earth that disappeared twenty years ago, leaving poor Moira practically destitute with a young son to look after."

"You know Moira Foster? From Park Avenue?" Tom asked, brushing away the spray of crumbs from the tablecloth before Mrs Puw noticed. Daisy nodded her head slowly, trying to recollect. She found smiling and nodding the safest way to continue the conversation instead of admitting when she had no clue who the other person was talking about.

"I wonder why he came back. Do you think someone upset about what he did to his wife killed him? I can't see why anyone else would want to murder him." Different scenarios flooded through her mind about what may have landed her with a dead man on her doorstep.

"Now don't you start that. You sound just like your aunt. There's actually a lot of people in the valley who would like to see that man strung up. When he went he took a lot of families' money with him, stolen from the Christmas savings club they used to run from the shop. He ruined so many Christmases that year. Now you leave it be and let the police do their job."

"Tell you something weird though right?" Tom said between mouthfuls of bacon sandwich. "He was in here yesterday. We've had some witnesses come forward and tell us so."

Daisy ran through all the faces that had been in yesterday, but there had been so many of them. Was it one of the tourist groups? They also had a few walkers in. Maybe it was one of them.

Then she remembered him. The one asking all the questions.

"What business did his family have?" A cold sensation ran down her spine.

"That's the even weirder thing. His great grandfather opened Foster's Haberdashers back in the 1860s. Their shop was next door. You bought it and knocked through."

"I spoke to him." She blurted out. Both faces stared at her, astonished.

"What did he say?" Mrs Puw asked. Tom sucked his thumb and wiped his hands on his trouser legs. Mrs Puw tutted, thrusting a tea towel at him.

"He ordered a pot of tea."

"But did he actually say anything to you?" Notebook in hand, Tom flipped to a blank page.

"Let me think. Oh, he asked about the shop. About when it closed and seemed really angry it had been knocked through." She tried to remind herself of their conversation as abrupt as it had been.

"Do you remember what time he came in?" Tom's pencil

flew across the pages as he took everything down, his eyes bright with excitement to have a lead on the information before the inspector.

"Well, I'm not really sure. He may have come in with the tour group at midday. But he didn't leave with them. I spoke to him after they had all left about 1pm. I offered him some Welsh cakes on the house, but he slammed the door shut and went up the footpath opposite." Daisy couldn't get the face of the man out of her head. The pale face as he lay on the floor soaked in his own blood. Could it really have been the same man she had spoken to?

"You don't remember what way he turned when he got to the top, do you?" She shrugged and shook her head.

"Sorry. I was clearing up after the rush and went into the kitchen with a full tray before he'd even got halfway up. I'm sorry, I think I will go have that lie down after all. My head is pounding." Tom flicked through his pages and opened his mouth to speak.

"No more Tom. Let her go to sleep. Maybe she'll remember something later after she's napped, but not now." Mrs Puw lay her hand on his shoulder and shook her head.

"Right. Yeah. I guess. I just wanted to know if he was with the group or just came in at the same time." He said, looking up at her innocently.

"Well, maybe you should go and ask the person who was the guide on the bus then shouldn't you?" Mrs Puw inclined a nod to the door.

"What? Oh! Mary. Yes. Yes, I guess I should." Hurriedly thrusting all his items back into his pockets and grabbing the last sandwich off the plate, he headed out with a wave.

"And you." She turned to Daisy.

"Yes, Mrs Puw. I'll go to bed. But you might as well go home."

"No, I think I'll hang round. I don't want anyone disturbing you. Besides, someone needs to keep an eye on that lot downstairs. I dread to think of the state they are going to leave it in. Don't you be worrying about me. I'll keep myself occupied." She knew that Mrs Puw was raring up to clean her flat from top to bottom, but Daisy couldn't argue anymore. The pain behind her eyes was blinding, and she just wanted to rest her head on her lovely, soft pillow.

Still fully dressed, she climbed under the covers, instead of the feather cloud she was expecting, her pillow felt like a brick to her poor, aching brain. The door clicked open and something heavy landed next to her, nuzzling at her hand with a gentle purr. She pulled the soft, warm body under the covers, grateful for the comfort and security.

Chapter Four

Daisy stood in her shop. The male voice choir in their black suits and white shirts filled every seat, a rousing rendition of Calon Lan made the air electric. Had they just finished a concert? Their burgundy bow ties hung loose at their unbuttoned collars. The matching cummerbunds, scattered in piles on the tables. On her knees, Daisy sobbed as she pressed onto the man's stomach, trying to stem the blood that pooled around her. Blood the same colour as his cummerbund and bow tie. She begged for their help as the song reached a deafening crescendo.

Gasping for breath and untangling herself from her twisted duvet, Daisy sat bolt upright. She looked down at her hands, but there was no blood. She pulled her glasses on, the fuzzy room coming back into focus.

It was just a dream.

Everything was as it should be.

Except for the song. The singing hadn't faded away with the wet warmth on her hands or the visions of the man dying in front of her. The words of Calon Lan filtered through the flat along with the smell of roasted meats. At her side, Barnaby stretched and rolled into the warm dent she had left behind in the mattress.

In the kitchen she was greeted with a sight that she believed could only be found in Wales. The land of song. Where impromptu singsongs could happen anywhere and everyone magically seemed to know how to harmonise. In all the years she lived and worked in London never once had a pub turned into a choir singing an old hymn, maybe the chorus of an eighties ballad but always out of time and tune.

Singing from their very souls were three of her closest friends. Mrs Puw, basting a leg of lamb as she leaned over the oven in a billow of steam. Michael, who stood at the kitchen sink peeling apples. Of course there would be apple crumble for pudding if Mrs Puw was cooking. Then finally Tom who, still in uniform, with a packet of smokey bacon crisps in hand, conducted from his usual place at the table. There had been a running joke about Tom's ability to eat his mother out of house and home yet still stay as slim as he had been as a teenager. His family had been teasing him about his "hollow legs" since his first growth spurt at aged 11. He had shot up 20cm during the summer between primary and secondary school and his mother had needed to return the as yet unworn new school shoes and uniform for a larger size in the last week of the holidays.

A shiver ran down Daisy's spine and the hairs on her arms sprang up as the final words of the song filled the air. Faces and voices raised to the heavens on the elongated final note, all three cutting off with perfect timing.

Canu'r dydd a chanu'r nos.

"Woohoo." She called out, clapping her hands with appreciation. The two men grinned like praised schoolboys, both bobbing their heads in mock bows. Mrs Puw shaking her head with an inaudible tut as she pushed the lamb back into the oven.

"Hey there sleepy head." Michael said as he plunged his hand into the sink to retrieve another apple.

"Make yourself useful and put the kettle on will you Tom? Wash your hands first, Daisy doesn't want crisp flavoured tea. Ych a fi." Mrs Puw slapped his hand away from the kettle. Tom rolled his eyes and shot a grin at Daisy but dutifully unbuttoned his sleeves as he went through into the bathroom.

"Are they still downstairs?" Daisy asked as she peered on tip toes down through the window. As she spoke the kitchen door opened and two forensic officers in their white paper suits stepped out carrying a box full of evidence bags. "Why are they coming out this way?"

"Tom said it's because they are still collecting evidence from the front door." Said Michael as he sliced. "They have parked all of their vans in the yard behind the old garage. He doesn't think we'll be back in the shop for a couple of days at least. But that means there will be officers front and back so at least you'll be safe."

A fleeting thought of annoyance at the inconvenience of the shop being closed was rapidly replaced with deep seated guilt for blaming the poor dead man for turning her day upside down by being killed.

"Any updates?" She asked Tom as he wiggled his clean fingers under Mrs Puw's nose for inspection before nudging Michael out of the way with his hip so he could fill the kettle.

"Not yet. DI Tyrant has taken over the station and my office I might add! He handed me a box with all my stuff and told me to find a desk somewhere else. Can you believe the cheek of it?"

"Tom. We know you're gutted about your office. He hasn't stopped moaning about it since he got here Daisy. But back to the important stuff yeah Butt?" Michael said handing Daisy a thick slice of apple.

Tom held his hands up in defence. "Sorry. It's just so humiliating having to go into the bull pen with everyone else.

Anyway we had a debriefing at lunchtime." Daisy glanced up at the clock and couldn't believe it. Almost four o'clock. Had she really slept most of the day away? "He's spoken to the wife, and the old business partner, they are saying they were asleep together at home. Ethan, the son, is away on business. We are waiting for a call back the last I heard.

"They deny having seen him since he left and that they were out all day yesterday. The boss is convinced they are telling the truth. Claims he 'has a nose for these things' but I'm not buying it."

"Why don't you believe them?" Asked Daisy taking a long slither of apple skin from the bowl, suddenly ravenous.

"I've knocked on every single door on Park Avenue today and at least four people saw John who knew him and three others who saw a man fitting his description. We all know Moira has barely left the house in years. So the chances nobody was home when he knocked was slim to none. Plus Bobby Brush said the Foster and Young's car hasn't left the street in over a week."

"Wait, Moira? Bobby Brush? Foster and Young? Who are all these people? Remember I didn't grow up here so don't have that inbuilt knowledge you valley folk seem to have about everyone.

"Twenty years ago, Moira Foster. Wait. Let me start right from the beginning." Mrs Puw sat at the table for the first time and poured herself a cup of tea. Never one for gossip, claiming it a sin, she had obviously been holding this tale in for years and nobody dared to interrupt her in case she stopped.

"John Foster's family had always owned the haberdashers and tailors. Moira had been a young girl when she was taken on just to man the till and cut fabric for the ladies, while old Mr Foster and John were out the back making their suits. They were sold in a tailors in Carmarthen and were really what kept the haberdashers afloat. When old Mr Foster passed away John took over the family business. But demand for bespoke suits was too much for one man and he struggled to keep up with the demand. Over the years, he had befriended a young man who worked at the Carmarthen tailors. He did customising of suits off the peg, taking in, shortening and the such. One day he appeared at the shop asking John to consider taking him on, that he would do anything asked of him to learn the full tailoring trade. The next day he started working and within a year he had bought the house next door to the Fosters."

Mrs Puw paused to take a sip of her tea. The time she took to place the cup gently back in the saucer and dab at her mouth before continuing lasted an eternity.

"Fast forward ten years and there were rumours going round that Lyle and John were having a bit of a disagreement. Apparently Lyle wanted to buy in to the shop as a partner, which would have given it the much needed boost as the tailoring side was bringing in less and less. Bespoke suit orders were dwindling with only a few London firms seeming to stay afloat. Lyle had lots of ideas for changes but John wanted to keep his family's business as a whole for the boy.

"The disagreement turned nasty with the two men refusing to even see each other. Which was difficult seeing as they worked together and lived next door to each other. So yes. Twenty years ago John up and left, wiping out the family's bank account as well as the business account. Taking all of the money from the safe while he was at it. Including the Christmas club savings which they had run for years.

"Moira was devastated. She was penniless and at risk of losing everything. She'd had to let the girls who ran the shop for her go and had to take Ethan, who was just a dwt, there every day. To be honest, I'm not sure how the shop kept going at all, apparently Lyle persuaded her to let him help, invested money. It did have a little revival for a while but a few years later the shop was closed. Lyle and Moira never officially became a couple, they lived separately until Ethan became an adult and Lyle moved into Moira's house to give him the opportunity to live with his then girlfriend, now wife." Taking a long deep breath, Mrs Puw looked around the table, "What?"

"Mrs Puw, I think that's the most I've ever heard you say in one go." Tom said digging his notepad from his pocket. "Why didn't you tell me this would be a whole history lesson I could have taken down notes. This stuff is like gold!"

Daisy laughed at the creases of concentration on his face as he scribbled away, his bottom lip bitten between his teeth. Mrs Puw, who seemed taken aback by her own outpouring of information, tutted but with a wry grin, gently clipped the younger man about the ear and returned to the oven with her back to the group.

"Do you think John came back to reclaim his family and Lyle Young took him out as retribution?" Michael asked. "He took this woman and child in when they were at their lowest. It makes sense that he'd feel like he'd need to protect them now incase John was attempting to hurt them again? Or wheedle his way back in."

Daisy thought back to their conversation. What had he actually said?

"He seemed more concerned about the shop being changed than about the people who ran it."

"I remember Ethan from primary school. He was always quiet and withdrawn. But then he went to the private school and he stopped really hanging out with any of us." Tom said not even looking up from his page.

"Maybe Moira was the one who killed him? What's that saying about scorned women?"

"Hell hath no fury like a woman scorned" Mrs Puw added without even turning her back on the gravy. "I remember Moira when she came to primary school. A right little madam she was by all accounts. She tied Elis Rowe's shoelaces together when they were waiting to go on as shepherds during the nativity when they were seven. But that doesn't make her capable of killing a man. Even if it was a man who left her with no money, gossiped about in the community and almost losing her child."

"Her child?" Tom's interest was piqued, his hand paused over the page.

"The social got involved. No idea who called them, but the rumour at chapel was that John reported her once he'd left town. She had no way of supporting Ethan unless he was in the shop with her all day. They were under the social for years after that but again I think Lyle had a lot to do with helping her there. It was his support and contributions that got them off her back in the end. Especially when he paid for Ethan to go to the private school." Mrs Puw dished up vegetables and meats onto the waiting plates as she spoke.

Daisy's mouth watered at the waft of roasted lamb and gravy as fully laden plates passed around the table. Her stomach gave a loud rumble, reminding her that besides the half a breakfast she'd had early that morning she hadn't eaten another thing that day.

The only sound for the next few minutes were those of knives and forks against the plates as they fell into silence. Daisy wondered if they were all running through the events in their minds just like she was.

Was it possible that Lyle Young had killed John Foster? It made sense that Lyle would be angry at how John had left Moira and Ethan. How easy would it be to kill a man by stabbing him? Could Moira have the strength to do that? From what she remembered of Moira, she was a slight woman. John was a big man and could easily have overpowered her. Then there was Ethan. He was bigger than his mother but was nowhere near as big as his father.

"Daisy. Daisy are you okay?" Images of two men fighting in her shop doorway swam from her mind and she looked first at the empty spoon in front of her face, then at the three faces staring back at her. Tom quickly moved his hand from her shoulder.

"What?" She asked surprised at the worried faces staring back at her.

"You've been sat there frozen with that spoon halfway to your open mouth for so long the custard fell off it." Michael said from his seat opposite her.

"Really?" She placed her spoon back into her bowl and smoothed her hair back "Sorry. I was just thinking about, well everything. It's been a strange old day." A feeling of heaviness seeped over her and she couldn't face the thought of another mouthful of Mrs Puw's coveted crumble.

"Come on boys. I think there's been enough excitement for one day. You've both finished your teas so let's leave Daisy have her evening back. I expect you need to get back downstairs Tom?"

"God yes!" He looked at the wall clock and jumped to his feet shaking the whole table while he did so. "I'd better get ready to start my shift."

"I'm in college tomorrow remember, but let me know as soon as we can get back into the shop and I'll help you clean it." Michael said to Mrs Puw quietly as he helped her put the dishes in the sink.

Chapter Five

Once again, Daisy was ripped from her sleep and sat up with a start. But the shouting of her dream didn't disappear. She rubbed her eyes, listening intently as she tried to reconnect with reality.

"Get off me. I didn't do nothing. Stop!" The male voice was familiar but in her half asleep state she couldn't pinpoint it, nor work out what on earth could be going on in the street below her window.

"Get him in the back of the car boys. Take him down the station." Without turning on the light Daisy pulled her curtains open a crack trying not to be seen from below. By the light of the streetlamp she watched as two uniformed police officers lead a hunched figure by his cuffed hands towards the police car. The window was open a crack so she could hear every word.

"Sir, I'm telling you that I don't believe Dafydd is responsible. Why are we arresting him?" Tom walked backwards into view, gesticulating wildly at Inspector Locke who followed him.

"Sergeant Griffith, he came back to the scene of the crime, with the potential murder weapon at 3am, why would he be here this time of night otherwise? Now let me do my job and step out of the way unless you want to be removed from this case?"

"But sir!' Ignoring Tom, the inspector strode past him. Tom dug his hands deeply into his trouser pockets and watched the convoy of cars as they led their way back up the valley until they turned up the hill towards the police station and disappeared. He glanced up towards her window, their eyes seeming to meet, even though she was sure he couldn't have seen her in the darkness of her room.

She watched him nod at someone out of sight and speak in quiet tones, before looking back up at her. He held his hand up and spreading his fingers out before walking out of view. It took a few seconds for his message to dawn on her. Five minutes.

It was closer to ten minutes when the back door creaked open and Tom, looking pale and tired, stepped into the dim light cast by the lamp on the corner of the work surface. He leant against the door looking a mixture of both angry and defeated and dropped his jacket down in a pile next to him.

"Are you on your way home or are you still on shift?" She asked holding out both the cafetière and the teapot. He glanced at his watch and pointed at the former. "The fire's lit, go and warm yourself up, I'll bring this through now in a minute."

Hands deep in his pockets, Tom was stood by the newly lit fire staring at the dancing flames. She had known Tom long enough to understand he needed to process things in his head first so saying nothing, she placed the tray on the coffee table and nudged Barnaby off the chair. He curled up on his bed next to the grate, but gave a her silent glare, meowed, then turned his nose up at her and lay his head down with a huff.

Sitting back in her chair she watched the bergamot scented steam of her Earl Grey tea swirling up into the cool room, the fire having not lifted the night chill quite yet. The deep furrow in his brow had told her there was a lot he needed thinking about, and things that he was none too happy about. She worried about him when he was like this and wanted to say something, check he was okay. But she was willing to give him all the time he needed, even if it was killing her.

"They arrested Dafydd Sparks." He said eventually, pacing up and down in front of the fire. Dafydd Sparks, or Dafydd Jones, had been the lead electrician at the pit head. He had taken the closure of the pits worse than most. He had struggled to find other work and hated taking any benefits, his wife passing away suddenly from pneumonia five years ago had been the last straw. He had barely spent any real amount of time in his home since. Preferring instead to wander the mountains and streets at all hours of the day and night. He was like a wandering hermit.

"It's not right. There's no way Daf did this. John was three times his size for starters. Dafydd says he's been with Farmer Madden helping with the sheep for a week. I'm not sure he was even in the village last night!"

Daisy slowly depressed the plunger and poured him a mug, adding four lumps of her best brown sugar, hoping the extra sweetness might help. She slid the mug across the coffee table along with the plate of biscuits.

"Come and sit down and drink your coffee. You're wearing a hole in my rug and you've almost stood on Barnaby's tail twice already."

"What? Oh, sorry Barnaby." He dropped into the matching wing back chair to her own and took the proffered mug swigging on the too hot drink with a grimace.

"Look, Tom, there's nothing you can do tonight. Dafydd will be left to sleep it off in the cells, and they will question him some time tomorrow. At most, you should pop into the station on your way home and give the inspector some insight into his history. Help them build up his back story so they understand him a little more."

"I guess. But the way the DI was talking when they drove off, seemed like he'd decided Daf was guilty before proven innocent. He even said that us village bobbies should watch and learn from those in the force who have dealt with more than petty pilfering and sheep worrying. I have a bad feeling about this Daisy, I don't like it one bit."

A flash of headlights crossed over the window and Tom raced to peer through a crack in the curtains.

"Bloody hell, that's the Inspector why is he back here again? I'd better get back downstairs. Thanks for the coffee and for letting me vent." Tom gulped the dregs of his mug, grabbed a handful of the shortbread rounds, thrusting them into his pocket before he headed for the door. He turned back to her "It'll be alright yeah? They have nothing on old Daf.'

"Go and speak to him. I'm sure he'll listen to you now they aren't rushing off with a potential murderer." Even as she spoke the words, Daisy had a strong suspicion that everything was in fact not going to be 'alright'. Her encounter with the inspector had given her the impression that he was just the type to get a quick answer and not worry too much about who he hurt along the way.

Daisy awoke with a crick in her neck and unfurled her body out of the chair. Her joints crunched and complained with each movement as she stretched herself to standing. Falling asleep in the chair had not been on top of her list of good ideas last night, but she had half expected Tom to return. She stoked the fire with new logs and pushed the poker until the embers caught the tinder and licked at the new wood. Barnaby gave her a small meow of appreciation before falling back into a deep snoring state, his tongue lolling out the side of his mouth. *Silly cat.*

Peering through the curtains she had expected to see some police cars, more forensic evidence collections, more investigating. But apart from a single officer the main road seemed to be quiet. The police obviously kept office hours unless it was an emergency it seemed.

As the kettle began to boil she wondered what she would do that day. Hand on the fridge door, she glanced at the calendar and swore under her breath. She was supposed to make the sandwiches and fairy cakes for the playgroup's teddy bears picnic. Yesterday had been filled with the shock of the murder. A pang of guilt hit her as she thought about the knitting ladies who had missed their weekly social's refreshments. She hadn't even thought about anything besides the shop. Would she be able to open today? Could she retrieve some ingredients and make the picnic here in her kitchen? She hated not knowing anything. But without Tom around how would she find anything out? Inside the fridge she spied the bacon and an idea began to form.

Tray in hand she made her way down into the back lane and through the small covered alleyway between her shop and the gift store next door. She had expected somebody to be guarding the back of the shop as they had been when she had gone to bed. Had they deserted the place now they had a suspect?

The sight of the blue and white tape blocking the pavement and the white tent over her doorway was jarring to see for the first time. The young officer standing watch looked barely out of short trousers to Daisy, but she was glad someone was still around or she'd have an awful lot of bacon sandwiches to eat.

"Good Morning Ma'am. I'm afraid you can't come through here. You'll need to go around." He stood to attention as she neared, sticking his chin out with determination. From his demeanour and his sparkling clean uniform, she guessed he was very new to the job.

"Actually this is my shop? I thought you might appreciate some refreshments? A cuppa at least?" She nodded down to the tray worried he may turn her away with an attempt at professionalism. But his whole body relaxed and a wide smile spread across his face.

"Oh lush. Thanks!" He stepped towards her but she moved back as he reached for a biscuit. He snatched his hand back, his eyes wide.

"You will only get something if you promise to never call me ma'am, or even Miss Fields again, unless your bosses are around of course. We don't stand on ceremony here. You may call me Daisy when it won't get you into trouble. Do we have an agreement?"

"Yes m….errr…" She raised her eyebrows "Daisy." He said with a toothy grin that showed the small dimple in his left cheek.

"There we go. That wasn't too hard was it?" She reached over the tape and placed the tray down onto one of the two outdoor benches that sat in front of each window. She reached her hand out "Very nice to meet you…?"

"Duncan. Duncan Grant ma'am, I mean Miss, I mean Daisy." His cheeks flushed as they shook and he quickly turned away to the tray.

"How long have you been out here alone Duncan?" Steam billowed into the cool morning air as he pressed the button down on the vacuum flask full of coffee.

"Since they arrested the suspect. Everyone else was needed back at the station so they left me here until the next shift comes. Sergeant Griffith said I was ready."

"Are you not here with the Cardiff contingent then Duncan?"

'Oh no, I'm from Gwynfu, I finished my policing degree in Swansea and this is my first posting. I've only been stationed here a couple of months. Mickey was so happy not to be the newbie any more!"

"I can imagine! I bet your mam is so proud of you."

"Oh yeah, first one in our family to go to uni. Some of Dad's lot ain't too happy of my career choice, but since he died we don't see much of them anyway. 'Dodgy dealers' Mammy always calls them." Daisy waited for him to swallow his mouthful of bacon sandwich before asking anything else, hoping she had softened him enough to push a bit harder.

"I hear they arrested Dafydd Sparks? I can't imagine he was even capable of walking straight let alone planning on killing anyone. Tom, I mean Sergeant Griffith seemed surprised as well." Duncan stared at her, she could almost hear his mind whirring wondering, what if anything, he should say. She didn't push, just smiled sweetly and wiped at a feather that had stuck to her window frame. It felt like an eternity before he spoke but her patience paid off. Duncan looked around him and leaned in closer speaking quietly.

"Seargant Griffith was so angry with DI Locke. I've never seen him so shocked. They didn't even question Mr Sparks. He was walking down the street and saw the police. He stopped to tell them he found a bloody knife in the park up on Ffordd yr Ysgol. He'd fallen asleep and it was on the bench next to him when he'd woken up apparently. Two of the Cardiff officers called the station and he was arrested there and then."

"But why would he tell them he'd found a knife if he was the murderer? Doesn't that seem odd?" She kept her voice low to match his.

"Yup, But DI Locke just mentioned something about the perp always coming back to the scene of the crime and that he was probably too inebriated to think straight." His attention was drawn by something behind her. He put the cup back down on the tray and hurriedly moved back into position at the doorway of the white tent and faced straight forward.

"Thank you for the breakfast Ma'am it was very kind of you."

Confused by his sudden change in demeanour Daisy turned and saw Tom, Inspector Locke and two uniformed officers walking down the street towards them.

"Miss Fields. You'll be pleased to know we have apprehended a suspect. If you could please refrain from disturbing my officers while they are on duty it will help us get out from under your feet much quicker." Inspector Locke waited for Duncan to raise the tape before ducking under. Tom exchanged a knowing glance with her as he followed.

"Of course Inspector. I was just bringing some hot coffee and breakfast to thank you all for your hard work. I hope there's enough for everyone but you know where I am if you need more. I just happen to have some unexpected free time on my hands." The inspector glanced at the tray and stared at her seriously.

"We are very grateful for the gesture Miss fields, but may I please remind you that this is a serious murder investigation and is nothing to made light of." He grabbed a bacon sandwich and drenched it in the homemade tomato sauce and turned away without another glance.

Of course not Inspector.

Chapter Six

The wheels of her little red cart clattered and bounced on the uneven surface of the lane, without the extra weight of the food she struggled to keep it in a straight line. She spied Tom's boots sticking out before she saw the rest of him stretched out on her steps, arms behind his head.

"Does your dad know that his favourite helper has escaped?" She said as she neared.

"He thinks I'm in North Field checking on the lambs." He kept his face turned up to the spring sun, eyes closed as if he had been asleep. Out of uniform he looked just like any other young farm boy in the valley. His boots were heavily caked with mud, his tracksuit bottoms were holey, baggy at the knees, and stained with motor oil. His t-shirt faded so much that Daisy could never have guessed at the band logo which had once graced the front or even its original colour. The t-shirt itself now being a vague grey.

"And why aren't you in North Field checking on the lambs instead of making my steps look untidy?"

"Where have you been?" He asked, ignoring her question.

"I had to take a picnic up to the library. Life doesn't stop just because I can't get into my shop and those teddies needed their finger sandwiches."

"Well I guess you'll be happy to get these then won't you!" Tom, finally opening his eyes and, sitting up, held up her shop keys, jangling them in front of her face. "Hey where are you going? A thank you would have been nice!"

Having snatched the keys from his outstretched fingers she abandoned her cart and ran to the kitchen door, swinging it wide with one twist of the key in the lock. Her heart dropped as she stepped into the dim room. Instead of the sparkling kitchen with its lingering scents of vanilla and butter, she was met with chaos. Flicking the light on just made it worse.

All her ingredients were still out of the cupboards where she had placed them the morning before, apart from those that had been on the island, those had been dumped in random places around the room. The police had obviously been using the island as a work area. There were bits of tape, torn scraps of paper, empty take away cups and even some empty evidence bags strewn across the surface.

She followed the path of dirty footprints through the beaded curtain and almost cried at the sight of her beautiful shop in a state of complete disarray. Tables and chairs had been pushed to the perimeter of the room and piled haphazardly onto of each other. The police debris cluttered the floor and every available surface.

"They don't tidy up after themselves?" She asked Tom who had wandered in behind her. She turned in a circle, her arms wrapped around herself. There was so much to do, the job seemed monumental, "And why were they even dusting for fingerprints in here? Nobody came inside." She ran her fingers through the dark dust on her till.

"Can you be 100% sure of that Daisy? Let me ask you one question the inspector didn't ask you." Tom walked over to the front door and unlatched it, pulling it open wide. "Are you in the habit of leaving the outside gate open when you lock up?"

A cold chill ran down her spine like a trickle of icy cold water. Why hadn't she realised before? She always locked the security gate that led into the little space that was once a communal porch for both the shops, but now just lead to her own door.

"I thought as much. Do you know who has a key to both the gate and the door?"

"Just me and Mrs Puw. Oh, I think Mrs Roberts might have one for emergencies that Aunty Poppy gave her years ago. But I guess..." Her mind drifted back to the renovations of the shop. "The security gate is the original. I guess whoever had a key to the haberdashers could still have a key? But they couldn't have gotten inside, it's the original door, but that lock is new."

"If you're sure you locked the gate, then either John had a key, or his killer did. We both know Dafydd would have no reason to have a key to either of the original shop doors or the gate. But they did find keys on him when he was arrested." As he talked, Tom grabbed a chair from the top of a table and flipped it to stand on its feet.

"Well of course he doesn't. Has anyone at the station actually checked the keys? Oh leave those." She said as he reached for another chair. "The floor needs scrubbing before they go back anyway. I'll give Mrs Puw a call, you know how much she loves a good cleaning session!" Daisy felt an urgency to get back outside, to warm herself in the spring sun. The dirt, the mess, the keys, it was all a bit too much.

"Cuppa?" She called behind her as she left quickly, trying to avoid looking around her any more.

"Iesu Mawr, I can't believe they left this place is such a state. Didn't their mothers teach any of them to leave a place as they found it?" Mrs Puw, who was wearing a housecoat that was likely older than Daisy, yet had zero stains, carried the large bucket of dirty water through the kitchen and out the back door.

"I'm sure a mop would have been perfectly sufficient to clean the floor Mrs Puw." Daisy called out to her as she placed the large tub of baking powder into its spot on the shelf. She heard the water splash over the floor followed by the tap being turned on. Mrs Puw returned to the kitchen wiping her brow.

"Nonsense. You can't get all the grime out of a floor with just a mop, they need scrubbing by hand at least once a week." Which caught Daisy by surprise. She turned and faced the older woman, her brows furrowed.

"Mrs Puw. Do you mean to tell me that on a Saturday evening, when you come to give the shop 'a good once over ready for the week' that you're actually scrubbing the whole floor by hand?" She asked astounded at herself for being so blind.

"And deep clean all of the ovens and kitchen surfaces, including the cupboards. It's no less than I have always done." She reached back through the door and retrieved her now full bucket. "No cat, you cannot come in here, you know the rules. No pets in the shop, now scoot." Barnaby mewled a long pitiful meow.

"Anywho, we can't dilly daddle, there's work to be done. Give me half an hour to finish in here and we can have a cuppa while the floor dries. Then you can put all the tables back in their places while I scrub in here. This is the best floor, the tiles really gleam when they are done." Within minutes she was back to singing one of the old Welsh hymns she always sang when she cleaned and Daisy hummed along as she wiped down the now empty surfaces, knowing that the chances were high that Mrs Puw would come along and scrub them later anyway.

Coming back into the shop a second time had been just as much of a shock as the first. She picked out all the issues she had missed the first time round. Mrs Puw had stood stock still as she took in the sight, but never one for outward displays of emotion she had simply taken a deep breath and tied a scarf around her hair.

"Well, let's get a wiggle on girl. It's not going to clean itself" She said, almost as if she'd accepted the challenge and was looking forward to tackling the monumental task.

With every surface, except for the kitchen floor gleaming they took their cups of tea and sat outside on the bench to take advantage of the clear blue sky and the warm sun. So often the skies were overcast or the sun was so low it was hidden by the mountains, this was a rare treat to catch it at just the right time.

"I don't feel right sitting out here doing nothing Daisy. What will people think?" Mrs Puw looked uncomfortable as she looked up and down Commercial Street.

"Mrs Puw, you are wearing working clothes and have been scrubbing the shop for hours. Everyone will have seen you're cleaning up a storm and know that you deserve a break, just like anyone else." Daisy leaned back and closed her eyes.

"But out here? Why can't we sit out the back? Look, Mrs Williams in the wool shop is looking over."

"Because the sun isn't out the back. The sun is here and we deserve to enjoy it." Daisy placed her cup and saucer back onto the tray between them with a little more energy than she had planned, sending a large slosh of boiling hot liquid splashing up over her thumb.

"Ouch." She shook her hand trying to cool it down then said "let's just enjoy the warmth and the quiet before the museum bus comes down. Then I promise we can go back inside okay?" Mrs Puw harrumphed, but closed her eyes and leaned her face up to the sun. Daisy smirked and wondered if this enforced rest break was the longest Mrs Puw had actually sat still in years.

"I've been thinking about that gate key." Mrs Puw said out of nowhere. Daisy, who had been lost in thought watching a bird circling high in the sky looked over at the older woman who had managed to stay still for all of five minutes and was now sat upright and facing her.

"What about the key?" She asked.

"Well, I know that the Fosters would have had a few keys. The security gate has been there since the shops were built, they all had them at one point, and Mr Foster's family were the first business in that particular shop. So with new family members taking over, plus spares for emergencies, there must be a small handful collected over the years."

"So you think Mr Foster was trying to break into the shop? But he wouldn't have gotten past the front door."

'No, but it's one of the original doors right? Maybe he hoped that the key still worked. He may have had a key to Poppy's too for all we know."

"But we had new locks fitted because the old ones didn't meet the insurer's standards."

"He wasn't to know that though was he?" With that, she stood, grabbed the tray and disappeared inside the shop just as the rumbling of the bus sounded in the distance.

Daisy ran her fingers over the keyhole as she pushed the door open, were there more scratches than usual? Then, shaking her head she locked the door behind her making sure the SORRY CLOSED UNTIL FURTHER NOTICE sign was stuck firm.

"Do you think he visited his family while he was here?" She leaned against the door frame as Mrs Puw stood waiting for yet another bucket of water to fill. Daisy spied the large block of old fashioned household soap and the scrubbing brush and wondered how Mrs Puw still had any skin left on her hands, and also whether she had a stock pile of that soap as Daisy was sure they had stopped making it years ago.

"You said he went up the footpath that leads up to Park

Avenue? Where else would he be going? I can't imagine he'd have had a nice welcome though. It practically put poor Moira into the asylum when he left."

"What about the man Moira married after he left?" Daisy asked trying to recall what she had been told the day before.

"Married? Oh no, love. She was never divorced. I don't like to gossip, but there were rumours in the early days that Lyle and her were together, which was frowned upon. But when the boy grew up, Lyle gave him his house to live in and moved in with Moira. That sealed their fate, the older generations weren't impressed, but by then standards of morality had changed and nobody under the age of forty batted an eye about an unmarried couple living together. But that was about the time Moira changed. She stopped going out, she used to be a regular here and then suddenly one week she didn't turn up and we never saw her in here again." As she spoke, Mrs Puw had moved her bucket to the side of the island and grabbed her brush and soap.

"Do you think he could have upset one of them enough that they would kill him?" Daisy asked. Mrs Puw sat up on her heels and thought for a moment, the water dripping silently from her fingers onto the floor.

"I suppose Lyle has always been known to have a bit of a temper, I've always thought he was a funny one too, never could take to him. Moira? I wouldn't have said so, but there's that old saying again 'Heaven has no rage like love to hatred turned, nor Hell a fury like a woman scorned'"

"And the boy?"

"He never really knew his father. I guess he would be angry at him, but he always treated Lyle like his dad and was very apathetic to any mention of John. Look. This shop isn't going to be open tomorrow unless we get a wiggle on. Let's finish up and then I have an idea to share with you that could help your little investigation."

"What do you mean investigation? I'm not investigating anything." Daisy said

"I know the look on your face. Poppy used to get exactly the same way when she perceived some injustice or another and could never let it lay until she had put things to rights. Besides. Dafydd is depending on you to prove his innocence. I don't trust that inspector as far as I can throw him. Now shoo." She waved her away before plunging her brush into the bucket.

Even watching her made Daisy's hands hurt. That water was straight from the outside tap and must be freezing!

As she carried tables and chairs, placing them in just the right positions so they would all fit, Daisy couldn't help think about everything that had happened in such a short space of time and poor Dafydd getting swept up in it all. She had no clue how she would be able to help, but she knew she had to try.

Chapter Seven

A few hours ago, the idea of bringing a meal to the grieving family seemed to be such a good idea. But now, standing on the pavement in front of number nineteen Park Avenue, Daisy second guessed herself. A flurry of nerves churned in her stomach, and she had to resist the urge to turn on her heels and scarper.

Oh, get a hold of yourself, woman

She had delivered many a meal to the grieving families of the valley, but never had they been for the estranged family of a murder victim. A murder victim who had been killed on her doorstep, nonetheless. She gripped the handle of her basket and pushed through the creaky front gate. Park Avenue was a desirable street to live on, the houses slightly larger than the usual miners' cottages, having originally been for more affluent professionals.

Each house had a small patch of garden on either side of the path leading to the front door. In contrast to the neat lawns, trimmed hedges and bright pops of colour from the flower borders she had passed on the way up the street, number nineteen's garden was an unkept tangle of waist high grass and overgrown hedges

Daisy carefully manoeuvred her way around a bramble stem that had encroached onto the path, while avoiding the deep cracks in the concrete that sprouted weeds and dandelions. At the door, Daisy looked back over the garden.

What a shame, she thought as she picked out mature plants dotted around the edges. *It must have been a beautifully kept garden once.*

Taking a deep breath, Daisy lifted the heavy, rusted knocker and rapped on the door. With each knock, shards of faded, petrified paint that had once been bright red fell to the doorstep.

She waited a moment and went to knock again, knowing that in these three storey houses, if they were on the level down from the road, they may not hear the door knocking. But before the tips of her fingers reached the knocker, the door creaked open a few inches. A pale face peered out at her.

"We don't want to talk to anyone; please leave us alone." The door closed again with a bang.

"Mrs Foster?" She called through the door, "It's Daisy from the Tea Shop? I just wanted to offer my sincerest condolences for your loss and to bring you a meal from the Guild. I'll leave it on the doorstep, shall I?" This wasn't going according to plan at all. Why hadn't they discussed what to do if Mrs Foster and Mr Young refused to open the door? Seeing she had no other option, Daisy placed the basket in the shade of the small porch, tucking the tea towel snuggly around the dishes.

Mrs Puw's words rattled through her mind "Make sure you get them to put the casserole in the fridge right away. The last thing we want is for them to get food poisoning and for us to be arrested for murder too!"

She had to hope someone would grab the basket as soon as she left. She hesitated to knock again, but thought better and turned to leave.

"Miss Fields." The voice boomed out of the open doorway

before she got halfway down the path. "You'll have to excuse my wife. Bit of a nervous disposition, you know, and all the police visits have been a little much." The man filled the doorway, in both body and presence. He ducked as he stepped out onto the doorstep, his arms open wide as he gestured her inside.

"Come in, come in." He beckoned, grabbing the basket from the step, a wide grin on his face.

"Thank you, Mr Young. I'm sorry; I didn't mean to disturb you. I just wanted to drop the basket off. The Valley Ladies Guild always brings something to grieving families. You don't have to invite me in." Daisy said the words while silently thanking the universe that he had asked.

"Nonsense." He said, almost grabbing her arm and pulling her inside the cool, dim passage. Daisy saw his smile falter as he looked back outside before slamming the door hard so that both the knocker and the letterbox rattled.

"Moira, bring the tea through to the parlour," he shouted down the stairs as he ushered her through the first door on her right. Mr Young hovered for a few seconds before muttering something under his breath, leaving her alone.

The parlour, traditionally kept only for important visitors like the vicar, or the queen, looked like one of the display homes she had seen at St Fagans National Museum of History. Everything from the original open fireplace, with its black, cast iron surround and the carriage clock on the mantle, to the heavily patterned wallpaper was immaculate. Not a speck of dust or a cushion out of place. But everything seemed sterile and perfunctory. There was nothing personal, no photographs or sewing box, no fresh flowers or magazine.

Nobody had ever invited Daisy to sit in their parlour before, so maybe this was normal? It made her feel both nervous and honoured, not daring to sit in either the armchair or the small sofa for fear of disturbing the crisp, white lace antimacassar and arm covers.

Hushed voices travelled up the stairs and through the closed door. Daisy panicked and edged nearer the window. A flustered Mrs Foster followed Mr Young into the room carrying a full tea set that would have felt at home in Daisy's collection at the shop. The tiny blue flowers on the white background rattled as she lowered the tray to the coffee table. A slosh of milk from the small jug filling the holes in the lace doily beneath.

"I'm really am sorry to disturb you both. I only wanted to pass over the basket and to ask if there was anything I, I mean The Guild, could do to help at this difficult time?"

"Nonsense, please sit down." Daisy perched herself on the edge of the chair facing the couple, who seemed just as uncomfortable as she did. "Pour the tea, dear."

"Sorry, yes of course." Mrs Foster's hand reached up to her necklace in an unconscious movement and shifted forward. Daisy's fingers covered Mrs Foster's as she took the shaking cup and saucer, their eyes met and Daisy couldn't help but feel that Mrs Foster was silently trying to tell her something. But the moment passed fleetingly, and Mrs foster's eyes dropped to her hands as she placed them back in her lap.

Daisy's mind ran amok with all the things she wanted to ask but shouldn't while trying to grasp for something she should actually say. She sipped her tea to make the silence less awkward struggling not to let the fact that she had scalded her tongue reach the rest of her face. Mr Young was the one to break the silence.

"So, it was your doorstep the old man died on then?" Daisy's cup shook in her saucer, sending tea sloshing over the brim as Mrs Foster took a sharp intake of breath. "Oh, come now. We all know that is why you're here. Some feeling of guilt? Charity? Or just pure nosiness? If you have questions, ask away. We have nothing to hide, do we, dear?" Mr Young nudged Mrs Foster's arm; she shook her head and smiled at him wanly.

All those questions were now screaming in her mind, and she closed her gaping mouth quickly.

"Please, I really am only here to pass on my condolences and bring the basket of food as we would do for anyone who has had a family member pass on."

"Nonsense." There was that word again. Why was everything nonsense to this man? "We'll give you something to gossip about with all those old biddies. That man ruined my poor Moira."

"Lyle, please," Moira whispered.

"No, Moira, people need to know. Do you know he left her destitute and caring for Ethan, who was just a tot? We haven't seen John for years, and I, for one, am glad someone offed him before he could come and upset things all over again. More than that coward of a man deserved."

"He didn't come to see you?" The words were out of her mouth before she could stop herself. Moira glanced quickly at Mr Young before shaking her head quickly.

"I'm so sorry Mrs Foster—"

"Please call us Lyle and Moira. Mrs Foster just adds insult to injury." Lyle interjected.

"Of course, and you can call me Daisy. I really didn't mean to upset you, Moira. Yes, John died on the doorstep of my tea shop, so maybe I feel a little responsible, guilty even. I just wanted to check you were both okay, really. I expect the police have been here a lot?"

"Yes, they were here for hours. Wanted to have a family liaison officer stay with us. But we didn't need that. That man was no family to us," said Lyle, slurping loudly at his tea.

"And Ethan? How has he taken the news?"

"He doesn't know yet. He is away on business. Took Hannah with him a few days ago. He's always travelling for work, so he must have wanted to take her along for a treat. I expect he's gone to London so she can shop and sightsee while he's working. He doesn't really remember John anyway.

"He sent Ethan a letter on his 18th, but he knew what had happened when he was a baby and returned it to sender. He had no more time for that man than we did." Daisy glanced at Moira occasionally while Lyle dominated the conversation. She seemed on edge, almost pained by his words. Daisy decided Moira must be suffering more grief than she was letting on. And why shouldn't she? John had been the love of her life once, the father of her child.

"I can't imagine how hard it must have been for you, Moira. I truly am sorry if I've upset you." The silence was maddening as the three drank their tea. Daisy couldn't stop herself from asking the one question she desperately wanted to know the answer to, and she tried to sidle around the subject.

"I found out that your old shop was one half of my tea shop today. I mean, I must have known it was before. I've been coming to the valley since I was a child, but it hadn't clicked in my head until someone mentioned it. Would I have known you when I was little, Moira?"

"Yes, I remember you sneaking across to us and being fascinated by the buttons. We had an 'bits and bobs' tin; random buttons that were only really any good for spares. You would sit with it behind the counter and look at every single one of them like it was a precious jewel." A glint of a smile appeared on Moira's face as she spoke. A hint of a memory struggled to resurface in Daisy's mind.

"I think I remember that, and maybe ribbons?" Moira chuckled at the mention; she seemed lighter, her shoulders straighter.

"Your aunt was always telling me off for spoiling you, always putting ribbons in your hair. But I never got a little girl of my own, and your curls were irresistible; they still are. You'd wander between the shops when the gate had been locked at the end of each day. You'd sit on my cutting table and let me fashion your hair in all manner of ways; you were always so patient."

The gate, this was her in.

"I forgot the doors were opposite each other. I remember sitting in the porch when the gate was closed with my dolls while Mrs Puw and Aunty Poppy cleaned. That gate must be very old."

"Oh yes, it's the original. There's only a few left on the street now."

"I bet they all have had so many keys made over the years that they probably aren't even very secure anymore."

"Oh, no, my dear. Haven't you ever tried to get a duplicate? They only provided a handful of those keys per gate, five per shop, I believe? Well, that's what I was told. We lost one of ours and couldn't ever get another made. They were handed down with strict instruction to never have more than one leave the house at a time!" Moira seemed much brighter speaking about the shop. It was as if she remembered happier times and Daisy was glad she could give her back those memories, and gained some new ones of her own. But the information about the keys was interesting. Had Aunty Poppy been given next door's keys when she bought it? Did she dare ask if they still had one? Or if John had taken one with him?

"Let me just go and grab that basket for you." Lyle stood, breaking the spell. Moira visibly shrank back to her former self; all the joy in her eyes was gone once again.

"Oh my, I really should be going." She glanced at her non-existent watch. Moira led Daisy to the front door as Lyle disappeared, his heavy footsteps echoing on the bare stairs down to the kitchen. Moira pulled the inner closed. They stood close together in the passage which was barely big enough for them both and the shoe rack. Daisy turned to face Moira, up close she could see pain in her eyes.

"He wasn't always a bad person, John. He was the most kind and caring man I knew, and generous to a fault. Would give you the coat off his own back. Something terrible must have happened to make him do what he did." As she spoke she reached up and gently freed a lock of Daisy's hair from a large, round button of a greatcoat that hung on the peg. Daisy held the coat still, the lion face on the button inches from her eyes as Moira's deft fingers made quick work of releasing her.

"Are you okay, Moira? Is there anything I can do to help?" Daisy grasped the older woman's hand before it could flutter back to her necklace; the cold, nimble fingers clutched at hers. Her hand snatched back at the sound of heavy footsteps.

"Here we go. I popped some of my veg from the allotment inside. Overrun with runner beans, courgettes and tomatoes we are, so always glad to find a new home for them." The basket piled high with vegetables was even heavier than when she arrived.

"Thank you so much; that is very kind of you. These all look wonderful. Actually, I have a lovely recipe for courgette cake I've been meaning to bake again." She smiled and turned to leave. She could feel them watching her as she neared the garden gate.

She turned back, Lyle's smile immediately returning to his fallen face. "I appreciate it might be uncomfortable for you, but I would love for you to visit the teashop, on the house of course. You are welcome at any time. There is always a pot of tea and plenty of cake options every day." Except today, she thought.

"We'll see. Bye now," Lyle waved. Moira nodded, and they disappeared inside with another loud bang of the door, which echoed down the empty street.

Chapter Eight

Daisy wandered down the steep narrow path between the houses, not even looking as she crossed Grange Street, the road halfway up the hill between Commercial Street and Park Avenue. Of course, with the adults at work and the children at school, there were barely any cars to worry about at this time of day. Not that the street was ever particularly busy.

The only thing she could think about apart from the weight of the basket was the key in her hand. Admittedly, it was an unusual looking key, but it had never crossed her mind it was anything special. Aunty Poppy had never told her to be careful with the keys, or how it was impossible to get a new set. Perhaps Moira was mistaken, and it wasn't all that difficult after all.

Stepping out onto Commercial Street, she looked across to the tea shop where she could see Michael replacing tablecloths and table centres. His face lit up in what she imagined was a loud laugh, sending a slip of hair down over his face. He swept it back as he turned and walked towards the kitchen.

Was he having a laugh and a joke with Mrs Puw?

She desperately wanted to nip across and put the basket inside, but instead of crossing, she turned left. Lamenting the thought of her little red cart sitting in its spot under the steps as the weight of the full basket grew heavier by the minute. But she needed to speak to someone before she went back, knowing she would be asked a million and one questions.

"Daisy! What a terrible thing to happen right on your doorstep. Come in, come in." Felicity Yarrow, owner of the Wick and Wax candle shop, ushered her through the door, with a swish of teal and gold. She looked like a bohemian princess; the long ends of her brightly patterned hair wrap lay over her right shoulder, co-ordinating perfectly with her long, loose, flowing dress. The potent mix of essential oils, the warmth rising from the vats of melted wax and the thrumming instrumental music piped into the room made Daisy's head spin. She placed her basket down on the floor and rolled her shoulders to ease the pain.

Born in the gardener's lodge at the edge of the Ty Melin Estate, Felicity, Flick's, childhood had been an eclectic one. Her parents being head gardener and house manager at the Manor House, Flick had been cared for alongside the family's children by the nanny and governess. But where the Probert children had all eventually gone off to boarding school, she had attended the nearby comprehensive. This left Flick in the unique position of being neither of the village yet never being able to truly be apart from the valley either. She had left for university at eighteen, worked a highly paid job and travelled the world. But soon after her fortieth birthday, the call of Penbodlen and family ties had grown stronger, bringing her back for good.

"That must have been such a shock to discover a dead man." She mouthed the words "dead man" silently as if they were dirty words that might pollute the air. Daisy had once seen Flick cleansing the space with a bundle of sage following an argument between a young, betrothed couple about the colour of candles they wanted for their table centres. The groom-to-be expecting they would both want the cheapest white. The bride-to-be collapsing into tears at the idea, having her heart set on dusty blue to match the bridesmaids' dresses. Flick had closed the shop as soon as they had left, not wanting to risk the bad energy permeating the "bones" of the building.

Daisy pulled her keychain out of her pocket wanting to avoid getting pulled in to any gossip.

"Can I ask you a question about your security gate, Flick?"

"My gate? Yes, of course. What did you want to know?" Flick did little to hide the confusion on her face.

"You share your gate with the shoe shop next door. Do you have many keys between you?"

"My keys? Is that what happened? Was the man stabbed with a key?" Flick's hand fluttered to the crystal at her neck.

"What? No! John —"

"So, it was John Foster! Mr Metzger the butcher said it was, that he was breaking in, unable to deal with the guilt of what he put his poor family through."

"I don't know what he was doing at the shop, Flick." Not wanting to get drawn into a gossip fest, Daisy tried to draw the conversation quickly back to why she had come in. "Flick, do you have all the keys for your gate?" Fishing in her pocket, she pulled out her keyring and held up the largest, heaviest key.

"Yes, of course I do. Well, Nigel next door obviously has his own. What is all this about keys?"

"Have you ever got them copied? I was told they were difficult to get spares."

"No, I just go down to Mick the Boot whenever I misplace mine. He makes a copy within a few minutes; he keeps a spare of all my keys because I lose them so easily. But my gate key doesn't look like that." She pointed a heavily bejewelled finger at Daisy, rummaged under her counter, muttering as she placed various rocks, scraps of fabric, oddments of metal clips and small brown bottles on the counter before smiling and holding up a small, shiny key.

"Oh, that's not the original!" Daisy's face dropped as she

looked at the key that could have belonged to any front door in the valley.

"I have no clue, sorry. This was the one I was given when I bought the shop. The lock looks old enough, but I guess it could have been changed years ago?"

"I guess." Daisy felt deflated. She wasn't sure what she expected to learn from this endeavour, but on her way out she peered down at the gate lock. Sure enough, there was the square mount just like hers, but in the place of her cross shaped keyhole, there was a round barrel housing a standard keyhole. From the number of coats of paint over the rusty gate, it looked like it could have been there fifty years at least.

"Thanks Flick, hey why don't you pop over when we are open again? We haven't had a proper natter for a long time." She waved back at Flick, who was tossing all the items back under her counter. Daisy often wondered how such a free spirit could have once been a successful lawyer.

Stepping out onto the busy pavement, Daisy pondered her next step. She found herself being swept along with a group of tourists with heavy Irish accents as they made their way down the street. As the group slowed to look into the window of the grocers Daisy was deposited next to the doorway, the cold metal of the gate brushing her arm. The circular lock was the same as The Wick and Wax, but much newer going by the lack of paint. Pulling ahead of the Irish crowd, Daisy walked along one side of the street, staring at each of the locks on the gates that remained. Most had been replaced over the years; a few, like the sandwich shop and the gift shop, had relatively new owners, and she figured they would have no clue about the keys.

But the bakers was a different story. The Brodbeck family had moved to the area with the sinking of the first pit and the influx of workers and their families. They had fed people through the many mining strikes, providing free bread for the soup kitchens, giving away any imperfect loaves to the cold and hungry children that turned up at the back door. If she had a chance of anyone knowing something about the keys, it would be Oskar Brodbeck.

The tinkling of the bell, the waft of warm air made Daisy feel like she was stepping back in time. With the rounded glass protecting the many cakes and pastries, the shelves on the walls filled with baskets of bread of various shapes and sizes; everything was exactly the same as it had been when she was a child.

Mr Brodbeck waved from his spot in front of the old slicing machine, a paper bag in hand as he waited for a cottage loaf to drop. He nodded his acknowledgment of her wave, and she stood to the side waiting for him to finish serving two ladies that Daisy recognised from the library book club.

Daisy loved this shop. She breathed in the fresh, yeasty goodness, recalling the feel of her nose pressed against the glass as she decided which treat she would buy with her hard earn wages as a child. Her wage being a shiny fifty pence piece on a Saturday morning after she had helped Aunty Poppy wipe all the tables and fill the bowls with the roughly hewn lumps of sugar during the week.

"Daisy, my dear. Here, your favourite!" Mr Brodbeck plucked up an ice cream cone filled with piped marshmallow covered in chocolate and handed it to her proudly. "Freshly made this morning." Daisy could feel the heat tint her cheeks, unable to hold back a small moan of delight as she took a bite of the gooey, sweet goodness and crunched the hundreds and thousands sprinkled across the top.

"That there is childhood in one bite, Mr Brodbeck." She wiped at her lips, afraid of the inevitable white moustache that usually accompanied enjoying this particularly sticky treat. Mr Brodbeck ducked under the counter and reappeared next to her, embracing her in a long, caring hug. His arms, strong from kneading, gripped her.

"And how are you, my dear? I heard, and I am so sorry that

happened to you. I was going to come over later to check in on you." He said, holding her away from him and checking her over from head to foot as if to secure in his mind that she was unharmed.

"I'm okay, thank you, Mr Brodbeck. I have a question for you though, and it's a bit of a weird one." There was no need to beat around the bush with Oskar. He was as straight as a die and nothing ever phased him.

Within ten minutes, Daisy and Mr Brodbeck were squeezed into the small back office surrounded by every piece of paperwork the shop had accumulated.

"This is the oldest paperwork. The family just kept buying new ones whenever a cabinet got full! But anything to do with the building of the shops and the keys would probably be in here." Mr Brodbeck banged his hand on the oldest filing cabinet in the room, sending a puff of flour into the air.

"I think you might need another office, Mr Brodbeck." Daisy laughed as they stood in the small rectangle of space between the desk and the door. The increasingly more modern filing cabinets that lined the walls made the tiny room even smaller.

"Mandy does it all on the computer now! We are going up in the world, Daisy. See!" The Brodbeck's youngest daughter had just finished a computer programming degree and would probably not be impressed that the brand new laptop, which her father proudly pulled out of the top drawer of the newest filing cabinet, was already covered in flour and doughy fingerprints.

"Look, we even have the internet down here with this little disk thing!"

"That's fantastic! I bet it makes life so much easier than worrying about finding everything."

"Oh, I don't know, Daisy. I always knew where I was with my ledgers and a calculator. Mandy says the spreadsheet will automatically calculate things, but I'm not convinced I trust it."

The bell from the shop rang out, followed by loud chattering. The group of Irish tourists had found their way across the street.

"Thanks, Mr Brodbeck, don't let me keep you. I'm not really sure what I'm looking for, anyway."

Alone, Daisy turned full circle, staring at the piles of papers on the desk, the filing cabinets and the shelves filled with thick leather-bound ledgers and dated filing boxes. It was like an archaeological dig through the history of a single shop, and a tingle of anticipation rang through her. Even if she learnt nothing that could help her, she was excited to dive into this valued archive as well as spend some time thinking about anything other than the murder for a while.

Daisy pulled open the heavy wooden top drawer, revealing thick folders filled with papers wedged in as tightly as they would fit. The musty smell of old books gave her a pang of nostalgia as she ran her fingers along the spines reading the dates written in fine neat handwriting. She pulled open the next drawer. The dates going back further, everything covered in a fine layer of flour, it seemed nothing ever changed with the Brodbecks. Sitting on the floor, she opened the bottom drawer, but instead of the neat bundles, it was overflowing with papers shoved in willy-nilly.

This is going to take forever, she thought as she plucked the top piece of yellowed paper and flattened it out against her leg to reveal an invoice for grain to be milled and delivered as flour.

Figuring the information she needed was at the bottom, Daisy quickly sorted the paperwork into piles of invoices, letters and miscellaneous paperwork, the dates slowly creeping towards 1889 when she knew the street began to be built.

Finally, two-thirds of the way down the drawer she found a receipt for the outfitting of the shop, nearly there thought

Daisy rushing through the next inch of papers until finally, there was a letter from a bank regarding the original mortgage for the property.

Roof.

Windows.

Carpenters.

Security. This was it! She pulled the final papers into her lap and riffled through them, pulling out anything that could be to do with the gate and the keys. At the bottom was a stack of large white envelopes tied together.

With stiff legs, she dragged herself up into the desk chair and read through each crinkled sheet, her heart racing. There was paperwork from the company called Meddalfa Metals for the construction and installation of the gates, and finally letters, quotes and invoices from Aubrey and Sons Lock Works. She read down the initial letter, her heart beating hard and fast as she skimmed with words jumping out at her. Innovative, high security, new unbreakable design. Attached to the back with a rusted staple that had stained the paper with a bloom of brown was a leaflet showing an expanded diagram of the internal workings of the lock, and there it was. The special key.

Not that she could see what was special about it. Daisy placed the letter to one side, hoping for the next thing to be The One. But all that remained in her pile were the envelopes. Deflated, she sat back in the seat and stared at the dappled pattern of the Artex ceiling.

Had she wasted the last hour for no reason at all? At least she had sorted that bottom drawer, so it was no longer a mess. Daisy pondered why it was so different compared to the rest of the paperwork. The only reason she could think of was that Mr Brodbeck's great, great grandfather had probably moved here before the rest of the family, and when the then Mrs Brodbeck had eventually arrived and taken over the office side of the business she had kept it neater.

Oh well, she'd better get back to the shop and help finish up for tomorrow.

She grabbed at the first envelope to put everything back in a neat pile, succeeding only in sending an avalanche of thick letters and folded plans across the desk as the ribbon untied.

She grabbed at the pile as it teetered over the edge of the desk, threatening to fall to the floor. They were plans for the village. Plots for the roads and houses. Solicitor's letters. Large contracts on parchment that opened up bigger than the desk, the writing loopy and decorative and mostly in Welsh. There were even what looked like machine plans. Probably something to do with the mine.

"Mr Brodbeck," she called through to the shop, quickly returning the sorted piles of paperwork on the floor back in the drawer and collecting the earliest ones on the desk along with the envelopes "Do you mind if I take these to look over? I promise I'll bring them back when I'm finished with them, and I will look after them."

"Of course, Bechan. No rush, they haven't been out of that cupboard for more than a century. I'm sure I'm not going to need them anytime soon."

Chapter Nine

"Mrs Puw?" Daisy called as she stepped inside the shop kitchen, the pile of paperwork clutched in one arm, the basket in the other, which was now laden with iced buns and a loaf of bread balancing precariously atop of the vegetables.

"Don't you step one foot in here, missy." Mrs Puw came running through the beaded curtain, waving a polishing cloth in front of her. Daisy stepped back outside with a start. "It's all clean and shiny. I don't need your fingerprints on anything, do you understand?"

"But—" Daisy started, wishing she could just put something down.

"Just for today, Daisy Fields, will you go home and leave the place sparkling for me? The tables are all set out ready. They have freshly ironed tablecloths. The cutlery is sparkling, the sugar bowls are full, and it all looks beautiful. I just want to savour it for today. Okay?" Daisy opened her mouth to object, but before she could speak she was being ushered out of the doorway as Mrs Puw replaced her indoor shoes. "Go up and put the kettle on then! I want to hear about your afternoon while I make your tea. Looks like you've made a few more visits than expected." She said, nodding at the overflowing basket as she pulled off her housecoat.

"So what do you think you can learn from all this?" asked Tom, who had appeared in the kitchen as if drawn by the boiling kettle.

"Probably nothing of importance to the case. I think the key thing was probably a bust, but these looked really interesting. All about the start of the building works in the village and the purchase of the land, I think. If nothing else, the history society should see it."

"So what did Lyle and Moira have to say? Did you speak to Ethan?" Mrs Puw said, her back turned to them.

"Ethan doesn't even know, apparently. Has been away for a few days on business with his wife."

"And they haven't even told him?" Tom gave her a quizzical look as he dunked a biscuit into his tea.

"Nope, apparently he had little time for his father, so wouldn't care to know." Daisy stared into the steam as it swirled up from her mug. The bubbling of the vegetable soup and Mrs Puw slicing the fresh loaf of bread were the only sounds as Tom leafed through the papers and then started tapping away at the screen on his phone.

"That gate company seems to be defunct, but I think the lock company might still be going. Do you mind if I take some of this to the station? I might find some more information for you, perhaps even something we could use as part of our evidence somewhere. Maybe delay the inevitable for Dai? It's a long shot, no idea how it could possibly be useful, but to be honest I'll try anything right now."

"I can't see why not. You have to swear to get them back safely though; I promised Mr Brodbeck I'd look after them."

The noise of the immersion blender in the saucepan signalled an end to the conversation, and they moved everything to the safety of the sidetable to avoid the chance of spillage.

Freshly showered and wrapped in her fluffy pink dressing gown, Daisy settled down to watch some telly before bed. She flicked through the channels hoping for something to catch her eye, but nothing took her fancy. Then she tried to read her latest book, a historical romance set in the rolling Yorkshire Dales. The duke racing across the county to stop the arranged marriage of his one true love. She had been riveted, barely able to put the book down when she had first started reading it a few days ago. But now, the horse jumped the same hedge three times before she realised she was reading the same paragraph over and over.

Something was niggling away at her, and she couldn't put her finger on what it was. Had she forgotten something? Was she supposed to do something this evening? Be somewhere? Giving up, she decided she would just go to bed early.

"Barnaby?" She called out of the back door, shaking the tin of treats that was guaranteed to get him running, "Come on, puss cat. Barnaby, it's bedtime." The fence rattled, and Barnaby's face appeared in the grass across the lane. "Good boy, Barnaby." She shook a few of the tiny fish shapes into her hand and held them out, but Barnaby stayed put, crouching in the shadows. "Come on, cat I haven't got all night." Barnaby slunk low to the ground as he crossed the lane, lit only by the lights from the windows and the moon. Then without notice he hissed and ran screeching down the lane.

"Barnaby, what are you doing?" Daisy ran barefoot down the steps and followed the dark shape of her cat. The hissing and yowling continued, followed by a scuffling noise that disappeared off into the darkness. Barnaby, noticing her nearing him, gave one final hiss and then slunk back towards her and brushed around Daisy's feet, nudging at her legs as if herding her back inside.

"Okay, okay. I'm going! What was that, hmm? Was it that big fox again? Or the Willis dog trying to wind you up?" Barnaby and the Jack Russell that lived in the flat above the builder's merchants were sworn enemies. They had more arguments than most humans she knew, but Daisy was sure they had never even got within six feet of each other, only ever growling and hissing their disapproval of the other's existence whenever they inevitably met. She peered into the darkness but couldn't see anything other than the empty lane and the long grass fluttering in the breeze.

In the brightly lit kitchen, Barnaby hopped up onto a dining chair and then up onto the sideboard, meowing loudly for his treats. Daisy dislodged the pile of papers from under him and then placed the tiny biscuits in a pile. Barnaby pawed at each one suspiciously before deeming it safe enough to eat.

Deciding she would make some Camomile tea to take to bed, Daisy pressed the button down on the kettle and began leafing through the smaller documents from the envelopes. There was a copy of the original sale of land from the farmers to the Probert family, who had built the Ty Melin Estate. She recognised the same surnames that were in the village now, some still farmers. The plans for the streets and the geological records for the sinking of the mines.

Daisy delved deeper and deeper through the history of the village until she came to a stapled stack of papers pertaining to Commercial Street. Contained within was a plan of each store that was being opened. She glanced over the names of the shops. Surprised that some used to be large single shops before being separated into two smaller halves. There was the Brodbeck's store sharing the larger space with the greengrocers, both still occupying the same shops now. Her eyes fell on the outline of her own tea shop, surprised that it had originally been one single store. So it had been split into two smaller stores before Aunty Poppy opened it up again?

Did she know she was restoring it to its original state?

The numbered list of names was fascinating. There was Brodbeck's; the greengrocers belonged to a Mr Granger and Sons; she wondered if they were related in any way to the Brown family who owned it now. And there, at number 32&33 was Foster and Young's Haberdashers.

Foster and Youngs.

Youngs? As in Lyle Young's great grandparents? Daisy's mind whirred trying to work things out. But Lyle and John had only met as adults and gone into partnership. So how had their grandparents been working together all those years ago?

"How do we know they were relatives of Lyle though, Daisy?" Tom said from the speaker on her phone. She had the camera scanning the list so he could read the names. He frowned as he tried to read the words. She flipped the view so he could see her face. She had called him as soon as she'd read the names on the list, partially to check she was seeing what she thought she was, and partially because she needed to tell someone immediately. She'd never have been able to sleep otherwise.

"How much of a coincidence can it be that someone with the same surname owned the shop with John's great grandparents? I'm sorry, Tom, I know you have a cynical viewpoint on most things. But this is too much. It must be. Look here. There's a name. Dylwyn Young of Carmarthen. Can you look into him?"

"I mean, I can try. Have a look and see if there is anything more to go on, maybe? What I don't understand is why all that information is in the Brodbeck's office? Like the stuff about the gates and the sale of the land to the Proberts. Why don't they only have what's related to their own purchase?"

"I think... Well, I don't know. It looks like it was all set up as a cooperative? I'm not sure though. I haven't read everything, and it seems like some bits are missing. But yeah, I guess it would make sense that everybody would have the information if the owners all went in on purchasing their plot to build their shop? Or maybe Mr Brodbeck was the spokesman or something?" She failed to stifle a long, loud yawn.

"Why are you awake anyway, Daisy? You're normally in bed by now." The background behind Tom showed him walking through the station back to his desk.

"What do you mean? It's only —" Daisy glanced up at the original black kit-cat clock up on the wall. The moving eyes seemed as surprised as she was to see that it was gone eleven. Bang goes that early night.

"I sat down three hours ago to wait for the kettle to boil. I guess I got a bit sidetracked!" She yawned again.

"Nos Da Daisy. Off to bed with you. Promise me no more sleuthing until tomorrow."

"I'm not sleuthing. But yes, Sergeant." She mocked a salute at her screen "Nos Da Tom," she said with another loud yawn.

Chapter Ten

Daisy rushed back and forth between the tables and the kitchen with fully laden trays. The shop was full of not only tourists, but villagers that hadn't stepped foot in the door for years, and each snippet of conversations she caught seemed to all be about the same thing.

As stressful as it was, she was grateful to be too busy to stop and get dragged into the gossip.

The tea shop had only been open half a day, but the thought of tomorrow being Sunday and the shop being closed was all that kept her going through the rush.

And why had she given Michael and Mrs Puw the morning off?

She took a deep breath, pasted a smile on her face and pushed through the curtain, coming face-to-face with DI Locke. Quick on her feet, she twirled past him, narrowly avoiding throwing the whole tray down his front. His surly demeanour never left his face as he watched her without flinching.

"Be right there Inspector, why don't you go on through to the kitchen? It's quieter in there!" She called back to him as she placed the tray down on the edge of a small table.

"Here you go, one ginger tea, madam, and here is your honey. This pot is your Earl Grey, sir. Enjoy!" She turned to walk away.

"Excuse me." She heard a finger click behind her and sighed.

"Yes, sir?" She turned back with the biggest smile she could muster. "Is there something else I can get you?"

"Sugar? I take sugar in my tea."

"The sugar is in the bowl, sir, right there on the table." She gestured to the small blue bowl, which the little finger of his left hand was touching. The man frowned at the pile of white sugar lumps. Harrumphed and waved her away with nary a thank you.

"I don't know how you can deal with that," said a gruff voice as she picked up the next order.

"I don't know what you mean, Inspector?" She said. Knowing full well what he was alluding to but not daring to let the negativity into her mindset.

"Well. Rude people like that. I don't understand how people can talk to others like that." Daisy tried her hardest not to smirk, recalling the way the inspector himself had spoken to her and his officers.

"Oh, you know. I just let it all go over my head. I don't take it personally. Maybe they are having a bad day and need a little kindness, don't you think?" Daisy walked straight past the inspector without a sideways glance.

"There you go. A tea party for three lovely ladies. Did you enjoy visiting the mine?" The two young girls who sat either side of their mother, eagerly grabbed at their gingerbread men.

"We went down in a big lift." Said the youngest, who was no older than four or five. Her mouth, full of biscuit.

"Jemima, don't talk with your mouth full!" Her mother chided gently, scooping crumbs off the tablecloth into her hand.

"Sorry, Mummy." She said, spraying crumbs down herself

again, then giggling. The poor woman shook her head with a long, tired sigh.

"I am so sorry." She said to Daisy, with a silent plea in her eyes.

"Oh, you're fine!" Daisy said with her hand on the mother's shoulder "The tea is going to be really hot for a little while girls, so why don't you go and play over in the corner while Mummy pours it out and keeps it safe while it cools? There are toys, drawing paper and colouring books!"

"Can we, Mummy? Please?" said the eldest, sliding to the front of her seat. Daisy thought the RP accent was the sweetest thing coming out of the mouths of such small girls. Daisy ran back to the counter and returned with a chocolate eclair as, holding hands, the girls shyly made their way through the room to the children's corner.

"Here, it looks like you deserve a little pick me up. Don't worry, it's on me." She said as the mother went to object.

"Thank you; you really are the sweetest. We have been travelling through Wales for a week with their father's work and keeping them entertained has been difficult."

"Well, they seem to have made a new friend now, so I'd enjoy the peace and quiet while it lasts!" Sat at the small white table in the children's corner the two little girls had joined a small boy in blue dungarees, their heads touching as they giggled at the book that lay open between them.

"I hope you don't mind that I helped myself?" DI Locke sat in the tatty old chair, a cup of tea in his hand.

"Of course not, Inspector Locke. I'm sorry you've had to wait for me." Daisy did mind that the inspector had potentially touched things in her kitchen with unwashed hands and made a mental note to wipe everything down once he'd left. "Did you need to see me about something in particular?"

"Ah yes. Seargent Griffith showed me some paperwork about the key to your security gate?" He placed his cup down on the footstool and pulled his notepad from his inside pocket. "The company almost went under in the fifties but has been limping along ever since. They patented your lock and key design a hundred and fifty years ago. It was supposed to be the next big thing in the lock world, I guess, but the blueprints were lost and they never really recovered." He slid the notebook back into the breast pocket of his jacket and took up his tea again, replacing it with his feet as he leant back in his seat.

"We called. Nobody has requested a copy of the locks for years, and they couldn't make them even if they wanted to, so the one Mr Jones had on him must have been an original."

"Thank you for telling me Inspector, is this the only reason you came here? To give me this number?" Daisy knew there must be an ulterior motive.

"Well no. I understand you got this information from the baker? I also understand that you were asking questions around the village. Even visiting Mrs Foster and Mr Young? You're not butting your nose in where it doesn't belong, are you, Miss Fields?"

"Of course not, Inspector Locke. I took a meal to a mourning family. The Valley Ladies Guild do it for anyone local who has a death in the family."

"Even an estranged family?"

"It isn't for us to judge who mourns, Inspector. Yes, Moira and John were separated, but he was still her husband and someone she had once loved. Plus, a young man still lost his father." The inspector furrowed his brows; Daisy tried to keep a respectfully neutral look on her face to hide the fact that she was very impressed by the excuse she'd managed to pull out of thin air.

"And the snooping around?" He asked, taking a sip of his tea.

"I object to its being called snooping around, Inspector. I visited a fellow shopkeeper and friend. I happened to ask about her keys after finding out how special they were. Then, realising most of them had been replaced, I visited another dear friend whose family had been an integral part of the planning and building of the village. It's lucky I did too. Did you know they were a brand new design when they were added to our gates? Perhaps there should be some sort of preservation order in place to ensure the remaining few are kept safe." Daisy was again impressed with her improvisation, but as she spoke she realised she was right. Perhaps the History Society should look into preserving the gates in their original condition.

The inspector got to his feet and handed Daisy his drained cup before straightening his tie. He gave her a long, loaded look.

"I don't think I need to tell you again to leave this to the professionals, do I, Miss Fields?"

"I wouldn't dream of stepping on anyone's toes." She smiled her sweetest smile as she spoke.

"I also hope that you aren't bothering my sergeant and trying to get information that shouldn't be shared? Because I will find out if there is a leak."

"I object to your insinuations. Tom is an exemplary officer and is a consummate professional. He works in the village he grew up in, policing his peers as well as his elders, and he manages to maintain a high level of respect while doing it. You may struggle to separate your private and professional life, but Tom Griffith certainly does not." Daisy puffed her chest out, offended on Tom's behalf that anyone would question his loyalty. Inspector Locke held his hands up in defence.

"I'm not insinuating that Sergeant Griffith is doing anything but his best, and I'm glad you seem to respect that. But I wouldn't be doing my due diligence if I didn't ensure other people weren't leaning on my officers for information." There was an awkward silence as the two of them stared at each other. "Is there perhaps any other information that needs sharing, Miss Fields?"

"No Inspector. Why would you think that?" Daisy thought about the papers that currently lay spread across her dining room table and all the notes she had made. Could he request to see her search history and find out she had been plotting Lyle's family tree before she came down to work that morning?

"Then I'll let you get back to your work." The inspector nodded and disappeared into the shop, shortly followed by the chiming of the bell.

Daisy went to the sink with the inspector's cup, realising as she did, that it wasn't the builder's brew that she expected of a police officer. She gave the light pink liquid at the bottom a sniff.

"That's so funny!" Mary called through to the kitchen from her spot on Daisy's sofa. "I never imagined the tough inspector would go for a cup of Peachy Princess Dreams."

"He would have had to choose it by the name on the front of the drawer too, which I find quite amusing." Daisy returned with two tall glasses of strawberry lemonade iced tea, the ice cubes clinking against the glass as she walked.

"I can't believe he was so rude to you, though." Mary took a long drink from the pink silicone straw in her glass and screwed up her nose "Ooh, needs some more ade to go with that lemon, Daisy." She shuddered, but still took another sip.

"It's perfect just as it is. It's your tastebuds that need to toughen up." Said Daisy, taking her seat, Mary's sweet tooth was well known to Daisy, who had already made the tea sweeter than she usually would. Mary stuck her tongue out before laughing and taking another longer draw of the drink.

"Right, missy, show me everything you've got so far." Said Mary, pulling up her feet and patting the seat next to her.

Shifting closer and pulling her laptop from the coffee table, Daisy went through all the things she had learnt about both the Foster and Young families. Using some genealogy sites, she had managed to trace the lineage right back to the first owners of the shop.

"Look, there's even a piece in the Gazette about the new village." She pulled up the article from her bookmarks and let Mary read about the cooperative that was pulling together to open up the new high street." See, it mentions all of the original owners, and here are John Foster and Dylwyn Young." Mary zoomed in on the screen at the pair looking proud as punch in their best suits and hats.

"Well, Lyle certainly won't be able to deny there's any connection, will he? Look!" Daisy pulled the screen closer to peer at the two faces. The one on the left shared a passing resemblance to the late John Foster, particularly around the eyes. But on the right. There staring back at her was Lyle Young's doppelgänger.

"It's like looking at a time traveller. It's uncanny." Looking at the smiling face made Daisy feel uncomfortable. She knew it wasn't Lyle there in the 1890s, but he was an exact copy of this man. "There's no way this could have been a coincidence, is there? No way he just happened to become friends and an employee of the great grandchild of his ancestor's business partner?"

"I mean, it may have been a coincidence they bumped into each other?" Mary said, chewing on a chocolate-covered strawberry, "but do I think the universe could accidentally lead to this? No."

"No," agreed Daisy. Shutting down the web page, not wanting to see Dylwyn Young's face anymore. "Come on, let's stick the film on; I don't want to think about dead bodies anymore."

"Ah." Mary grimaced and fished in her handbag, pulling out an old, battered VHS case.

"Really Mary? Dial M for Murder?" She shook her head but took the tape and crossed the room to the small television.

"I picked it up last week at the chapel jumble sale. I didn't know, did I?" Daisy looked back at her with a disapproving look, but broke into a grin.

"What's that look for?" Mary asked, a piece of popcorn midway between her bowl and her face.

"Oh nothing. I have just decided what we are watching next time." She plopped down into her seat and dug her hand into the large bowl of popcorn.

"You wouldn't." Mary said aghast as the pirating advert played on the screen.

"Oh, I would, Mary, I definitely would." Daisy laughed, running through all of her favourite musicals, deciding which one Mary would hate the most.

Chapter Eleven

Church bells pealed cheerfully through the valley, signalling the call to the Sunday morning service as Daisy walked up Ffordd yr Ysgol. The large stone building of the primary school that gave the street its name dominated this end of the street. The colourful designs in the windows, along with the playground equipment, looked silent and forlorn, waiting for Monday morning to roll around to fill it with children's laughter and joy once again.

Although she had never been to school here, she had visited it many times over the years. The original fittings, calling back to a different way of life, always amused her. The large open fireplaces at either end of the assembly hall, the separate entrances, yards and toilets marked "Boys" and "Girls". Her own primary school having been a brand new build on the outskirts of Cardiff, with all the mod cons of the day.

Further up the street was the park. In reality, it was a gap in the long terrace where three or four houses had been demolished because of subsidence, a real threat in these old mining villages. Instead of leaving the patch to become an overgrown eyesore, the mine, which had owned most of the land and houses at the time, had donated money for the men of the street to create a nice leisure space.

When she was a young child, there had been a small climbing frame, a slide that was so tall and skinny it would never pass health and safety checks today, as well as swings and two small rocking horses on thick heavy springs that the boys would use as trebuchets on each other.

She remembered the uproar when the county council condemned all these small parks and ripped out the play equipment. The villagers had petitioned the community councillors to keep the spaces usable, but only the benches, a large piece of grass in the centre plus some flower beds and hedges around the perimeter remained.

She had expected to see evidence of the police having searched the space. No remnants of tape. None of the grass looked over-trodden, nor the flowers trampled. Considering the mess they had left of the shop, she was surprised that they had left this outside area so pristine.

She walked up the steps and looked around her. Where did she even start? There were five benches in all. Two original ones at either end, another three newer ones running along the back edge which had been installed when the play equipment was removed to placate the villagers.

But which bench had Dafydd slept on? She could search the entire space, but having some clue of the killer's and Dafydd's movements would be a great help. She stared at each bench for a few moments before moving on to the next.

The old ones. It has to be.

The three new benches all had small curves of metal separating the long seat into three smaller sections. There was no way a fully grown man could sleep on them, no matter how inebriated he might be. Sadly, Daisy figured that was the exact reason they were built that way, hadn't she read an article on that very subject just a few weeks ago? Hostile Architecture she thought it was called.

So that left just two.

Walking to the nearest bench on the right side of the park, she couldn't see any signs of anything untoward having happened there. But what was she expecting to find? A note? A large pool of blood? Something to just jump out at her shouting, "hey I'm evidence!"

She slowly circled the bench, looking around her feet in case she found some sort of clue. But nothing magically appeared among the blades of grass. Again, she found nothing obvious. No sign of anyone having sat or slept there at all. She sat down heavily on the nearest of the newer benches and lifted her face up to the clear blue sky. Small clouds wafted their way past, and birds chirruped and chirped as they flitted in and out of the flower beds behind her.

Okay, Daisy, let's think about this again.

She pictured the route she had just walked from her shop. If the murderer had run this way, he probably wouldn't have even noticed anyone sleeping on this first bench as they passed. They should have noticed someone facing them, though. So that one must have been the bench where Dafydd was sleeping.

Following the same routine, she walked slowly around the further bench, leaning in close in the hope she would notice something, anything. Even the smallest piece of evidence, no matter how inconsequential it seemed, might be the very thing that helped prove Dafydd's innocence.

Was that dried blood on the seat? The wood was covered in so many stains and marks it was difficult to pick out how old things were, but there definitely seemed to be something newer than the rest, something raised on the surface. Digging in her pockets, she pulled out a sandwich bag. She always carried a few to place foraged nuts, berries or even wild garlic, then rooted through her hair for a clip.

Crouching down, she peered closely at the mysterious substance. She followed one drip where it had run down between the slats and had dripped onto the floor. She scraped at where the substance had congealed into a drop coming out from under the seat and placed it, clip included, into the awaiting bag. She pulled a pen out of her inside pocket and scribbled the date. Before putting the bag in her pocket she laid it flat again and drew a quick layout of the park and put a cross on the picture of the bench.

Loud squawks and rustling in the bushes behind her made her jump and lose her balance, falling hard to the floor. Crossing her legs, she looked around the park to see where the noise was coming from. There was nothing but a couple of crows having an argument in the hedge, flapping and diving at each other.

The crows carried on their loud fight, in and out of the hedge branches, partially hidden by the green of the leaves. What were they fighting over? It must be food or packaging some children had dropped in there.

Another crow came down and stood on the back of the bench closest to the ruckus and watched with his head tilted to one side. The new crow decided the focus of the fight must be a treasure, eyeing up his chance to grab at it. Mesmerised by his movements, Daisy watched him lean forward, his beak swaying as he watched for his chance.

He pounced.

Beak first and wings tight back, he glided the short distance, grabbed with his claws and flew away, dragging a torn piece of red cloth with him into the centre of the grass. The first two crows, shocked by what happened, swiftly followed and, instead of trying to regain possession of the cloth, picked a fight with the bigger crow. Wings flapped as the three circled each other, pecking and squawking.

But Daisy was no longer watching the birds. Her eyes stayed fixed on the red cloth as she quickly made her way across the grass before they remembered about it.

But it wasn't red cloth at all.

As she neared it, she could see it was a torn strip of what looked like part of a white t-shirt, the dark red looking very much like dried paint, or blood.

"Shoo, go on with you!" Daisy stomped towards the crows, waving her arms, placing herself between them and the fabric in case they decided to take another grab at it. The trio landed on the back of a bench, and now it was their turn to watch her intently.

She walked around the fabric while once again digging in her pockets. She pulled out another sandwich bag and, leaning it against her hand, did another drawing of the park and placed a big cross in the bushes. Using a twig that lay nearby, she scooped up the material and placed it into the almost too small bag, pushing it down with the end so she could seal it.

After walking up and down the perimeter hedges, pulling back branches and poking the ground with another, bigger stick, she determined there was nothing more to be found. The three crows, still on their bench watching.

"Thanks, guys, I really appreciate the help here." Daisy nodded and went to turn away. "Oh, here, have this as a thank you." A wax food wrapper appeared as if from nowhere. She opened it to reveal a fresh, if slightly squished, flapjack. Three sets of shiny, inquisitive eyes watched her break it and crumble one half at her feet. Without even waiting for her to leave, the birds jumped down and happily pecked through the grass to find their treat. "I think we all deserve this for a job well done!" She said as she mimicked a cheers with her own half and took a bite. There was a chorus of cooing and clicks as she walked away.

"You didn't bother getting anyone to look in the park where Mr Jones said he slept?" Standing on one side of the police station's tall reception desk, Daisy raised her voice in annoyance at DI Locke, who stood on the other side.

"Officers did a full search of the park and I can assure you that they would have sealed the area if they had found anything of importance." The inspector's face turned a bright shade of red. Daisy couldn't be sure if it was from anger or shame.

"Well, I think this, and this," she jabbed at each bag that lay on the desk between them, "might just prove that the officers you sent weren't up to the job, don't you?"

"Miss Fields, a random substance found in a place where drunks eat their gravy and chips doesn't really warrant sealing off an area for investigation." He held up the smaller of the bags and peered at the dark flecks and the hair clip inside and side eyed his sergeant, who was smirking from where he leaned against the doorframe into the back office.

"Okay, but what about the blood on here?"

"Hold on now, we have no way of knowing this is blood, or that it came from our victim, or that where you found it was where it was originally dropped. You say some birds were fighting over it? There is nothing to say it isn't some old painting rag that one of your little friends stole from a rubbish bin three streets away."

"So you're telling me that I have brought potential evidence and you aren't going to do anything with it?"

"Look, Miss Fields, I'll have another team search the park in case something was missed. I'll even send your evidence—" that last word said with a sneer that made Daisy clench her teeth until her jaw ached, "off for analysis. But in all honesty, I think you've wasted your time. Never mind, this will be a funny anecdote for me when I get back to Cardiff. Even if this was blood from our victim on the bench or the T-shirt, all that proves is that we have more evidence to point to Mr Jones being guilty."

"What? Wait!" But the inspector had already closed the door, leaving her alone with Mickey Schofield, the young constable who was manning the desk. "Grr, that man!"

"Sorry Daisy. I'll make sure these get bagged and filed

properly and sent off right away. I'll do it myself." It was only then that Daisy realised the inspector hadn't even taken her evidence with him. Had he had any intention of sending them off at all?

"Thanks Mickey. Say hello to Mammy for me."

"I will. She's a bit under the weather with a head cold at the minute."

"Call in on the way home. I'll get some of my fire honey and some Elderberry Elixir blend ready for her. Those will perk her up right away."

"Ah great, she's been sniffling for days. Oh, Daisy." He called after her, "Did you want your hair clip back when they are finished with it?" He held up the bag, which was now placed inside an official evidence bag, and pointed at the small black object. Surely he was joking? But there wasn't an ounce of jest on his face. "I have to put it on the form."

"No thanks, Mickey, I think I can let that one go!"

Chapter Twelve

"Now, Barnaby, you know Mrs Puw is going to be upset with me if you stay in the shop." Daisy grabbed Barnaby by his hips and gently dragged the big ball of fluff out from under the table in the bay window. He had made a beeline for a small hole in the skirting board and spent the last few minutes trying to fish something out from its depths. She scooped him up into her arms, ignoring the disgruntled growls and the ferocious frown he was giving her.

"I'm sorry, Barnaby, but out you go." He tapped her cheek with his paw to prove his annoyance before jumping from her arms and scarpering out of the back door with a yowl. She raised her hand to her cheek. Had that really happened? It had been a firm tap, and no claws were involved. But still. Her cat had just slapped her!

"I hope that darned cat hasn't been getting hair everywhere while you baked this morning, Daisy?" Mrs Puw's voice was quickly followed by her figure in the back doorway. The look on her face saying 'I'm not angry at you, I'm just very disappointed,' which always made Daisy feel worse.

"Of course not, Mrs Puw. He snuck in while I was getting some fresh air."

"Of course he did." Mrs Puw had no mercy for Barnaby, who had once left a collection of fur balls and a mouse tail hidden in the children's corner and was now banished.

"Everything is done." Daisy tried to veer the conversation swiftly away from 'that darned cat,' "the bread is still cooling, but all of the baked goods are in the display cases and I've topped up the tea caddies in the kitchen as well as the jars in the shop. What are you doing, Mrs Puw? I already swept right through."

"Do you want anyone to find cat hairs floating in their teacups?" Mrs Puw had grabbed the mop bucket and was filling it using the outside tap.

"But we are about to open up."

"Then you'd better start prepping the milk jugs and let me do a quick once over then, hadn't you?" She disappeared through the curtain. "Nefi blw, drycha'r blew I gyd. Duw Duw." Daisy's grasp of the Welsh language was tenuous, but she got the feeling that she'd be hearing about this for the rest of the day.

"Old Don James wants to speak to you, Daisy." Mrs Puw appeared at her side as she filled the sink with hot bubbly water. She loved her hodge-podge of mis-matched cups and plates, but she did wish they were dishwasher proof. Or that Mrs Puw would at least let her test some of the chipped ones to see how they fared.

"Old Don James? Why? I didn't do it." Daisy still hadn't forgotten the ear bashing she'd received after being chased from the James family orchard for scrumping apples when she was eleven. Her ears had rung for days after.

"Don't panic. I think he and Young Don are having an argument about something, and he wants you to put it right. Go on, I'll make a start on these; I know how much you love washing up." What on earth could Daisy know that nobody else in the group knew? Ushered away by Mrs Puw's flapping tea towel, Daisy took a deep breath to steel herself for a row.

This morning was Llun Lles, Wellbeing Monday, when the oldest members of the community were brought to the teashop between 9-11am to see each other and catch up on old times. This was something Aunty Poppy had begun when the shop expanded. Poppy had been part of the chapel's outreach for the elderly and would visit as many as she could each week. Although they loved seeing her and the other volunteers, everyone had been wistful about missing old pals.

A chorus of hellos ran through the crowd, and she greeted all of the faces who had seemed ancient even when she was a small child. Miraculously, some of them looked younger now than they had then!

"Will you please stop these two bickering, Daisy? They haven't shut up since they arrived!" Edith begged her as she hurried over, grabbed Daisy's hand and dragged her to the father and son duo who were now pointing fingers in each other's faces. Edith Dwight, manager of the Community Centre, was this week's volunteer charged with trying to keep the conversation from descending into rants about politics, religion or the miners' strike. Edith was a quiet woman who excelled at arranging events and activities such as senior lunches and the toddler's teddy bear picnics, but dealing with cantankerous old men with a bee in their bonnet? Not so much.

Edith was a quiet soul, however her fashion sense made her an icon in the village. She always dressed like she'd stepped out of a history of fashion museum; in fact, having been inside her house, Daisy thought she could actually open one in her own right. The three-bed terrace, in which she lived alone, was packed floor to ceiling with vintage clothing. This week, Edith was favouring the 1940s. She wore a burgundy swing skirt, a cream collarless blouse with tiny pearl buttons and sported the wonderful Victory Roll hairstyle and bright red lipstick.

"Now boys. Put those fingers away and hush. I don't want to have to separate you two. Now what is all this argy-bargying about, hmm?" Daisy quaked in her shoes as silence fell upon the room. She towered over the two men, hands on her hips waiting for the clip around the ear, but none came so she pushed on. "Come on now, tell me all about it. Nothing can be worth all this bickering, can it? You two have to live together, for goodness' sakes."

Old Don James spoke first. Going by the younger generations in his family, he must have been a full, well-rounded figure of a man in his youth. But now, well into his eighties, his hard worked body was thin and frail, bent from years of mining as well as running the farm.

"I told the boy here that this shop was once the haberdasher's, the whole thing. I remember getting my first pair of long trousers here. But he says it was two shops, half the haberdashers and half was a cafe. Later to be Poppy's place. You know Poppy?"

"She's Poppy's niece, Daddy, of course she knows Poppy!" Young Don James 'the boy' who himself was in his late sixties rolled his eyes at his father and shook his head with exasperation.

"Actually, you're both right." Daisy crouched down so the hunched old man didn't have to struggle to look up at her. "When you were young, Mr James, old enough to wear long trousers of course, the shop all belonged to the Fosters. Later, they sold half of the shop and just kept the one side." Expecting both men to be happy that they were correct, Daisy was surprised to see that they both in fact seemed equally annoyed the other was also right.

"Told you I was right, Boy!" said Old Don, turning the wheels on his chair to face himself towards the table and waving at Edith to refill his cup from the pot.

Young Don folded his arms across his chest with a sigh and stared out of the window. Daisy shrugged and smiled at the ladies opposite, who had been totally enthralled in the argument. Turning to leave, she felt a cold, arthritic hand slip into hers.

"Mrs Easterling. Hello, how are you?" At a hundred and three, Mrs Easterling was currently the oldest member of the community. To look at her, in her lilac jogging bottoms, the matching sweatshirt covered in an array of wildflowers, you'd be forgiven for thinking her at least twenty years younger. Even her hair was coloured with a lilac rinse, having never got out of the habit from when it was popular in the nineties. She waved her other hand at Daisy to lean in closer.

"That wasn't right, Cariad." She said, gesturing with her head towards the two elderly men who still sat practically back to back, ignoring each other.

"I'm sorry, Mrs Easterling, what wasn't right?" Daisy pulled up a chair to sit face to face with the kind woman who had once snuck her a buttermint during a particularly long chapel service.

"They were two families. The Fosters, yes, but also the umm…" She tilted her head to one side and closed her eyes as she thought, "O dammo'r ymenydd." She tapped at her head, frustrated she couldn't recall.

"That's right, Mrs Easterling. The Fosters and the Youngs. You knew them?" A prickle of excitement ran through Daisy.

"Mamgu was the canteen lady for the builders when they were building the shops. She told me they had built her a wooden shed, and this was before the track was run all the way up here, so they used to fetch her up from the train in the morning and take her back down in the afternoon. She knew all the shop owners and the builders, so they'd all call at the house even years later." She said with a proud smile on her face.

"Mrs Easterling, how are you getting home?"

"My Darlene is fetching me after her Zumba class, Bach.

Trying to lose a few pounds before her holidays, she is. Don't know why she's bothering though. She's going in two weeks."

"Do you think she'd mind waiting a bit? Once everyone's gone, I'd like to ask you a few questions if you don't mind?"

"Don't you worry about that. She'll do as she's told. She's a good girl is our Darlene." Then under her breath added, "Well, until this year she was, anyway."

Darlene, dressed in a matching tracksuit to her mother, only in pale pink, was standing looking over old photographs on the wall when Daisy came through with a fresh tray of tea and biscuits, a tattered old folder under her arm. Apart from a few regulars, the place was comparatively silent compared to an hour ago when the Llun Lles group was in full swing.

"Thank you so much for staying Darlene, I hope this isn't holding you up?"

"Oh, not at all, love, as long as you don't mind my niffing the place up a bit," Darlene said, wafting the neck of her sweater. Her face was pinker than her tracksuit, and a sheen of sweat sat above her top lip.

"Good Zumba class, was it?" Daisy asked, gesturing for Darlene to take a seat.

"Don't know why you're bothering with all that." Muttered Mrs Easterling as she grabbed a white chocolate cookie and dunked it decisively into her fresh cup of tea.

"As you so well know Mother, I'm doing it because Mamgu Morgan had a heart attack when she was fifty-three and so far you and I have avoided any major health issues by being fitter haven't we." She said through a fake placating smile and then quietly to Daisy "Mammy's been telling everyone I'm trying to get a 'beach body'. Iesu Mawredd, if my body isn't ready for the beach by the age of seventy-five, it'll never be ready. She's just annoyed I'm not taking her with me, but we tried, and the cost of travel insurance for her was three times more expensive than the rest of the holiday combined!"

She rolled her eyes in feigned annoyance, but a smirk edged her lips, and she shook her head as she patted her mother's shoulder. "But you're going to stay with Aunty Mabel down in Aberhenwr so you can have fish and chips and see the sea every day, and then we are all going to that fancy hotel when I get back, aren't we, Mammy? The one you like?" Mrs Easterling tutted and turned her body away from her daughter as she concentrated intently on her cup of tea.

For the second time that day, Daisy Fields felt a pang of loss for something she would never get to experience. First with the elderly father and son duo and now here with this argument between mother and daughter. She had no family that she could grow old with. Both of her parents had passed away many years ago; Aunty Poppy had died in her sleep. She had no siblings or cousins that she knew of.

At that moment, Mrs Puw decided it was the perfect time to wipe the already clean tables down and fill the sugar bowls. She was humming a well loved hymn as she worked. As she walked past their table, she reached out, pulled a single, lost curly hair from Daisy's sleeve, and a wave of guilt swept over her. She did have a family she could grow old with. Mrs Puw doted on her like a mother hen, making sure she ate and slept and always voiced her opinion even when Daisy didn't appreciate it. She had Mrs Roberts, Tom and Michael, Mary and all the other villagers who had loved and called Poppy their friend who looked out for her. They may not be blood, but they were definitely family.

Chapter Thirteen

Mrs Easterling hadn't really had anything new to tell her from what the bakery papers had shown. There were tales of arguments between the shop owners and the mine owners, very exciting historical information, but all learnt second or third hand and nothing that could help them now. However, within an hour of leaving, Darlene had arrived back at the shop looking even more flustered than earlier and a damn sight more grubby. She'd knocked on the window and waved at Daisy to come outside. Mrs Puw, who had been closest to the door, hurried out first.

"Darlene, what on earth have you been doing?" Mrs Puw had fussed at her friend, picking bits from her hair and dusting her down.

"Mammy had me up in the loft as soon as we got home, Olwen, then wouldn't let me change before turning right back and bringing these down. She thought Daisy might find something important in here." Then to Daisy, "She also told me to tell you something she remembered on the way home." She had pulled an old envelope from her pocket and read aloud, "Lyle's grandfather was a cad. The diaries explain it all." She had obviously read the look on Daisy's face "Don't ask me, I have no idea! But here, take these." She pulled open her boot, revealing three tatty cardboard boxes, one with photos and papers piled up and over the top. Then two that were filled with books.

"I'm so sorry Darlene, I didn't mean for you to drag back here. I would have come and got them from the loft for you."

"Oh, dim ots cariad." Darlene waved away Daisy's worries. "In fact, I should be thanking you; it's the first time in weeks she's had something other than complaints at me for deserting her! Actually, I haven't seen her as animated about anything for a long time!

"Martha, the girl who sits with her while I go shopping and helps me get her in and out of bed, has been keeping her up to date on all the comings and goings. She's Dafydd Spark's neighbour's niece, and they are all devastated. After everything the poor man has been through. Mammy is positively giddy she can tell Martha she has helped with the case."

Daisy leant into the boot to pick out the first of the boxes. But stopped as Mrs Puw placed one hand on her shoulder before waving across the road.

"Bobby, Iestyn." She called across the road.

"Yes, Mrs Puw?" Called the teenage boys in unison, riding towards them on their bikes.

"Take these boxes round the back and up into Daisy's kitchen for me, would you boys?"

"Of course, Mrs Puw." The two boys leant their bikes against one of the benches.

"Bechgyn dda. Come to the back of the shop when you're done and I'll get you both a nice treat." She said as they hauled the first two boxes out of Darlene's boot.

"Has anyone ever said no to you, Mrs Puw?" Daisy asked, watching them disappear through the little archway.

"Well, why would they do that?"

That evening, Daisy stared at the ever-growing piles of

papers and now books spread across her dining table and sideboard. She had discarded the first few years of diaries back into the boxes. Marianne Pritchard, as was, had begun her diary keeping at the young age of 16.

Expecting to see the trials and tribulations of a young working class Victorian child, Daisy had been surprised to see that each entry was in fact more like a journalistic report of the events of the day. But as yet, she had found nothing of substance.

But what was she expecting to find?

Beyond an interesting contemporary account of local history, surely there was nothing to actually be gained from these diaries?

So why did she keep on reading?

What was drawing her in?

Waiting for the kettle to boil, Daisy picked up the 1889 diary again and continued to read through each page until she finally found the first mention of the new village and the shops being built. She read well past the kettle clicking off, absorbing the fascinating details the young Marianne put into her entries. In another life, she could have been an investigative journalist. Perhaps if she had been born a hundred years later.

Marianne had written everything that she felt was important, or injustices done to others; even the smallest details mattered. Details like the fact that the Coal Board men, city folks in their suits and totally inappropriate shoes, would stand in the mud around her little hut talking down about the workers.

"They call our hardworking men country yobs and no good for anything, not understanding why they need to spend all this money to bring the families into the valley. Yet they seem to not realise that without the men who risk their lives at the coal face, there would be no pits and no reason to bring their families here in the first place. That bringing women will ensure the men are cared for and those families mean money. Money

that has created a thriving economy in the surrounding valleys."

"Well said, Marianne!" Daisy said aloud to the empty room as she closed the finished notebook. Marianne had upgraded from diaries to blank pages after the first year, which had been a gift from her aunt, allowing her to fill as many pages as she desired. This left Daisy with a lot of books to read, but it had taken her an hour sorting through each one to get them all into date order. For the second time in a week, surrounded by piles of musty old books and papers, she realised she enjoyed it so much that she might volunteer to help the History Society with its artefacts.

She reached for her cup of tea, realising that not only was it not on the table, but was still sitting next to the empty teapot and now cooled kettle. Pressing the button down to reboil the water, knowing that Mrs Puw would judge her harshly for not replacing the water with fresh, she stood staring at the blackness through the window.

A movement outside made her gasp, followed by the gentle rapping on the door before it creaked open.

"I swear you can smell the kettle boiling, Tom," she said to the grinning face that peered at her from the dark. "Why are you wandering around so late at night?"

"It's Monday, innit." He said, sitting down heavily in his usual chair nearest the door, pulling off his flat cap and rubbing his hands through his hair.

"Of course it is. And did you win?"

"Yup, we beat The Glyn Arthur Arms lot hands down." He said, with a huge grin on his face at the darts team win, which if Daisy was correct put them in the league's quarter final.

"And exactly how many pints did you have to celebrate your win?" She scrunched up her nose as she placed the biscuit tin and a pot of her sweet dreams tea on the table. The lavender, blackberry and fennel struggling to cover the smell emanating from him.

"What? Oh, don't worry, I only had two. I'm on shift in the morning." He unbuttoned his coat and shoved it towards her. She pushed it away just as quickly, the overpowering smell of beer making her nauseous.

"Dai Top got into a to-do with one of their players badmouthing the beers because his favourite wasn't on tap. There was a scuffle, and my jacket got covered."

"Well, at least put it outside so I don't have to smell it when I get up in the morning, yeah?" Dutifully, Tom leant back in his chair, pulled open the back door and threw the coat outside. Daisy shook her head and poured them both a cup of tea. Tom sniffed at the cup and wrinkled his nose but said nothing.

"Umm, Daisy?" He blurted out, looking around. "I'm sure your piles of paperwork are multiplying. What exactly is all this stuff?" Daisy blushed and ran her fingers through her hair.

"Mrs Easterling told me about her grandmother, who worked as a sort of canteen lady when they were first building the shops. These all belonged to her; they are her diaries."

"And how are these supposed to get Daf off for murder?" He asked, flicking through the pages of one notebook.

"Oh, I don't know!" She leant back in her chair, letting her cup clatter back into its saucer "But something keeps niggling at me, Tom. I know Lyle's family was involved in the shop back then. Is there any possibility that he doesn't actually know that? If he does, does Moira know? Does it even matter? What does any of that have to do with John's death, anyway?" She shrugged, her hands falling into her lap, defeated.

"Did any of the stuff I found at the park help?" She asked, looking up at him hopefully.

"Nothing has come back yet," Tom lowered his voice. Looked around him, as if someone may be hiding in her kitchen, and leant closer "But I do know the boss gave his officers a stern talking to. And by stern I mean we thought the glass in the door was going to give out!"

"But why?" Daisy whispered and leant closer too. Tom's eyes sparkled with excitement.

"He sent a team of his men to search the park, yeah? They went to the wrong one!" Unable to contain his excitement, he banged the table, making his cup jump in its saucer, and laughed before whispering again, "They went to the one on Fordd Ysgolig instead of Fordd yr Ysgol." He sniggered and shook his head. "But you don't know that, of course." His normal voice sounded suddenly loud, making her jump. He straightened out and took a glug of tea. "Why does this taste of what my nana smelt like?"

"Drink it. It'll help you get a good night's sleep." She said, taking a sip and breathing in the lavender steam. Tom took another mouthful, but seemed unconvinced. "Did you know they had been at the wrong place?" She asked.

"Of course we did. I tried to tell the boss, and the team who were doing the searching. But nobody wanted to listen to us. 'Just watch and learn, farm boy.' The sergeant said." Tom put on a deep, brusque voice as he mimicked the tall, gruff sergeant she had met a few months ago when she had helped solve the murder of the late Reverend Becker.

"I can just imagine. So how did they find out?"

"After you left, he was giving them a right old rollicking for missing vital information and was jabbing at the little map you drew of where you found the stuff. Sergeant Muscle was staring at it for ages, me and Mickey had bets on how long it would take them to realise. You could practically hear the cogs whirring and see the steam coming out of his ears as he looked at it."

"You really should have said something, for Dafydd's sake." She implored him, with a headshake of disapproval.

"Daisy, I really tried. I even marked it all on the big map, where Daf said he'd slept, right down to the bench he was on. Nobody paid any attention to it. Every time I brought it up, I was shot back down again. Besides, I was kinda hoping that their incompetencies might help Daf in the long run."

"So how long did Sergeant Muscle, I mean, Monroe," she glared at him as he laughed "How long did the sergeant take to realise the mistake?"

"I won the bet. Mickey was much more sure of his brain prowess and thought he would get it within half an hour. He stared at that map all through the row and for an hour after. It wasn't until he went and stood at the map that he realised something was up. But get this. He thought you had messed up, not him."

"The silly bint went to the wrong place, Boss. This place is nothing like the park we went to. Look, this one is half the size and isn't even a play park. Where she says this bench is, is actually a huge climbing frame." Tom mocked again. "They all had a good laugh at that until the boss finally asked me to point out where the place was that you had been."

"And that's when you told him the truth?"

"That's when I let him work out the truth. He asked why I had marked the places I had. I told him, because that's where Daf had been and the route he had taken. Daisy, it was all there, marked up for everyone to see, including the route he had taken to get to your shop. I hadn't hidden nothing."

Daisy sat quietly looking at him, trying to decide if she should admonish him for not trying harder to let the Inspector know that there had been a mistake.

"Oh, you should have seen the colour of his face, Daisy Chain,"

"Don't call me Daisy Chain."

"He was positively puce. Even his arms. He tried to blame me for the mistake, luckily I had plenty of proof, including the tapes of Daf's interviews where both of us specifically say Ffordd Yr Ysgol. I even got Dafydd to repeat it at one point. I also made sure both Duncan, Mickey and I wrote it down multiple times in our notes that we had tried to let them know, with the date and times. Even the paperwork for the search had the street name in bold, which I highlighted and underlined myself."

"Did you get in trouble?" Daisy felt sick to her stomach that either Tom or the two young constables would get disciplined. Tom was old enough to fight for himself, but she didn't want Mickey or Duncan getting dragged down with him. Tom reached over and patted her hands, letting his rest on top of hers to stop her wringing them. His hand was still cold from the night air. But sent a warmth through her.

"Daisy, we did everything by the book. Even if he wanted to punish us, the union would be on him like a sack of…well, you know what. Stop fretting. It's their mistake, and now they have to back peddle giving us an extra day before Dafydd gets moved to the big station in town."

"So we have until Wednesday?" She sighed. What could possibly happen in the next 24 hours that would stop Dafydd getting moved?

"We have until Wednesday. Don't worry, I'm sure something will come up. I have Mickey scouring through the records of anything to do with Lyle, Duncan is working on those keys and you…" He paused before standing "You do whatever sneaky magic you can muster up." He yawned and stretched.

"Do you want to sleep on the sofa? Save you walking all the way back home?"

"Nah, I'm on earlies and my uniform is all at home so I'd better be heading back. Besides your sofa is tiny, I don't know why you don't put a bed in that second bedroom. Then I could keep a spare uniform in there for nights just like this."

"Tomos Griffith, are you trying to sneakily wheedle your way into moving into my spare room?"

"No, of course not. I'm just saying it would be handy to

have a room that isn't halfway up the mountain, is all. Plus, I can't really bunk down in an empty cell when we have people here from town, can I, even if it does mean we have other people to share the night shift with."

Daisy watched him meandering up the lane. He would soon climb over the stile and take the shortcut up to his family's farmhouse until he disappeared into the darkness. She knew he had walked those tracks since he was a child and could probably do them blindfolded, but she still worried about him, especially when he'd had a pint or two.

Chapter Fourteen

Two for Tuesday. One of the busiest days of the week where Poppy's Tea Shop was usually full to bursting with visitors wanting to grab the bargain of two pots of tea for the price of one.

This was the one day of the week that Daisy allowed Michael to take on the baking and instead she spent her early morning measuring out tea leaves, flower petals, cacao nibs and so much more to create the blends that brought people back time and time again.

Aunty Poppy had been a true tea aficionado; she had been known to travel to far-flung countries on hearing of a special blend, or new style of brewing tea. She had once spent a month in India learning all about the different chai blends from various small villages to create her own perfect mix of spices.

Daisy had inherited that love of blending tea, but where Poppy would name her blends to show the contents and the possible benefits, Daisy had brought what Mrs Puw had coined her "big city flair" and began giving them fun names like her Arabian Nights, a blend of Lapsang Souchong, with orange peel and cinnamon. Or the ever favourite with the children; Magic Fairy Garden, Rooibos blended with rose petals, vanilla, butterfly pea flowers and raspberry, sweet and pretty in the pot, with a rosebud added to each cup, but totally caffeine free. The magic of the tea turning pink with a splash of lemon juice always drew a gasp of amazement from the awed faces.

She hummed as she filled the large canisters in the shop as well as the drawers in the kitchen. She and Michael wove their way around each other in a synchronisation that only two people who had danced this dance on many a weekly occurrence could.

"You know you should let me come in and do the baking more often. Heaven forbid you could even get a lie in some days, Daisy. Besides, look at you! You're in your element mixing those blends; I don't see your eyes sparkle like that when you're baking focaccia," Michael stood proudly surveying the day's offerings that sat cooling on racks around him. The yeasty smells from the bread and the sweetness of the cakes and biscuits made Daisy's tummy rumble, reminding her it had been hours since breakfast.

"You have more important things to worry about, young man. Like getting through college for a start?" She crossed her arms over her chest and tried to feign an air of authority akin to Mrs Puw.

"Getting through a course on baking, desserts and confectionary? I think time served can only benefit me, no?" Michael pushed out his bottom lip in a pout and fluttered his eyelashes at her. "Please?" He said in a sickly sweet singsong tone, sidling up to her and nudging her arm.

"Okay, okay, you can also bake Saturday mornings during term time, and in the holidays we can work out as and when." Daisy grabbed a small container and held it under Michael's nose. "Sniff it and start thinking of a name." Leaving him standing with his eyes closed and his nose deep in the glass, she added hot water to the teapot and let it stand.

"I guess I do enjoy all this. It's a bit like making potions."

She stared around at the beautiful creations Michael had baked that day. She did also love baking. Most days. But it had become to feel very much like a chore. Aunty Poppy had concentrated much more on the tea and sweet treats. The bread, and only ever sliced white loaves, having been bought from the Brodbecks. Now, they used a minimum of three types of bread a day. Michael had obviously been bitten by the bread bug this morning as there were no less than five types of bread! There was the ever popular oat bread, the basic white cob, his new favourite cheese and tomato bread and even a pile of soda farls.

"Barley Sugar!" Michael's loud voice made her jump and clasp at the edge of the work surface.

"Barley..? What are you shouting about?" Why was she being so jumpy recently?

"The tea! It smells like the Barley Sugar sweets they sell down at The Sweet Spot. Very sweet and caramelly with a hint of lemon."

"Oh, right? Sorry, of course." She poured them both a cup, and they both stood there inhaling the steam. "Yes, I guess I can see what you mean" she blew the top of the scalding liquid and sipped carefully.

"Hmm. That's disappointing." Michael furrowed his brow after his first sip. "That doesn't quite hit as I was expecting."

"No." She walked across to her 'Cabinet of Creations,' as Michael liked to call the Welsh dresser where she kept all her ingredients. "But I think I know what's missing." She grabbed the pot containing palm sugar and sprinkled a tiny pinch in each of their cups.

Michael took another sip, and a smile swept across his face.

"Yes?" she asked tentatively, taking another sip of her own

"Yes!" He nodded his head enthusiastically and patted her on the shoulder. "Make a small batch and we can push it with my orange and lemon cake. I think they'll pair really well together. That sweetness along with the tang."

Daisy didn't have any time to comment on the fact that Michael hadn't, in fact, made an orange and lemon cake. He was already humming happily and pulling fresh lemons and oranges from the bowl, smelling each one in turn.

"What on earth have you two been up to?" Not wasting any time for formalities, Mrs Puw was already at the sink washing her hands before Daisy had even realised she'd come in, changed her shoes and hung up her coat.

"Bore da, Mrs Puw." Michael grinned as he measured out butter. "Our clever Daisy has made another wonderful tea recipe."

"Don't you bore da me, young man. You are here to help on Tuesdays so everything is done and set up for opening time and edrych." She pointed to the clock on the wall. "Five minutes until that door is supposed to be open, and you are both faffing around and nothing is even put out in the cases yet let alone the kitchen set up ready." As she spoke, she tied her apron around her waist and grabbed a display plate and carefully began moving the miniature Black Forest cakes from the rack, each one with a cherry atop a swirl of perfectly piped cream.

Daisy, knowing it was best to say nothing, went back to her tea area and, with the help of her trusty calculator, began mixing up a whole batch of the new tea blend adding just the right amount of palm sugar to add a hint of sweetness. She was adding a blank label when Mrs Puw appeared at her side.

"The doors are open, and Mr and Mrs Parker are here wanting toasted teacakes and a pot each of Earl Grey and Buttermint." She gestured with her hand for the container took a sniff. "Barley Sugar?" She asked, cocking her head to the side.

"Yes! Do you want to try some?"

"In a bit. I want to be able to enjoy it right proper." And with that she was off, and Daisy knew they were okay.

It had been a busy morning. The three of them carrying trays laden with pots of tea, flying in and out of the beaded curtain as customers came and went. By 11am, Daisy had to force Mrs Puw and Michael to take a break.

"Look, once these two trays are out, everyone is served. The Jones' Top Road and The Jones' Butchers are all set, so you make a pot of that new tea for Mrs Puw to try, Michael, and I'll clear up a bit in here. No arguing." She carried a tray laden with two large scones, pots of clotted cream and strawberry jam out to a waiting table. The two pots of tea, one Peachy Princess and the other she thought might be Caribbean Sunset from the smell of the coconut and orange scented steam that clouded her glasses.

"Ah, good morning, you two. I haven't seen you in a while." She said to the two smiling women. Marla Jenkins and Barbara Jones worked down in the sewing factory and liked to meet at the shop when their shifts allowed.

"We had a big order in a few weeks ago." Said Marla moving things around the table so everything could fit.

"We've been run off our feet, working all hours!" added Barbara. "Them up in the office should really come down and try making a skirt in the time they give us."

The two fell back into their well-earned rest and catchup as Daisy wandered back to the kitchen, pondering the Jones surname, when the bell rang. "Take a seat I'll be right there." She called back without looking.

Growing up, she thought it was odd that so many families were named Jones, yet most of them were unrelated. It made sense people had to tag on an identifier, yet it seemed so difficult to shake it once you had one. Jones the Butchers were still called that even though the family hadn't been in the butchering business for at least three decades!

She came back into the shop with her final tray, looking around for the newcomers. She struggled to stop the smile on her face turning into a look of shock as she spotted the last people she had expected to be in that morning.

"Here you both go. A pot of breakfast tea for you, Sheila, and my extra strong Builder's Brew for you, Jean, and two of Michael's soda farls. I wasn't sure which jams you wanted, so I brought a selection." She took a deep breath and walked towards the table of three sitting in the window, having barely glanced at two of her regulars as she'd served them.

"Lyle, Moira, how lovely to see you again." She turned to the third person sitting at the large table and smiled expectantly.

"Daisy, this is our son Ethan." Lyle introduced the man who was the spitting image of the young John she had seen in her photographs. Was that a flash of something on his face when Lyle called him 'our son?' Whatever it was, it was gone in an instant, and Ethan held out his hand for her to shake.

"Nice to meet you, Daisy. My mother has been telling me about the shop. I hope you don't mind if I have a look around while I'm here? I haven't been inside since I was a very small boy."

"Of course, feel free. Now what can I get you all?"

"What are they doing here?" Michael whispered, peering through the curtain as she pushed inside the kitchen and began preparing the tray, which she had once again assured them was on the house.

"They are here to drink tea and eat cake, Michael. What else would they be here for?" She tutted at him.

"I don't know Daisy, seems a bit suspicious if you ask me. Why would they sit at that big table? And why is Ethan wandering around tapping on the tongue and groove?" Mrs Puw joined him at the curtain, and she had to clear her throat to move the two of them out of the way to get back inside to retrieve the cakes.

"Will you two go away?" She hissed as she carried the tray back over to the table that seated eight. Ethan was now looking at the cases that displayed her cakes. Not at the cakes themselves, but at the cabinet. Running his fingers over the metal edging that held the glass in place. She tried to ignore him, but her face must have given away her confusion.

"Don't you worry about him, dear; he's always had a fascination with old things, hasn't he, love?" Lyle pulled Moira into a firm side-hug. Moira, looking uncomfortable, gave Daisy a small smile and nodded.

"Thank you so much for the tea and cakes Daisy, you really don't need to."

"It's the least I can do. I'm glad Ethan is able to reacquaint himself with the old place."

"Ethan, stop fussing over there and come and drink your tea." Lyle's voice boomed across the quiet murmuring of the shop, drawing everyone's attention towards them. Moira shrank into her seat, Ethan's face flushed red, but Lyle didn't seem to even notice.

"Actually, do you mind if I join you? I was about to have a break, and there's a few questions I had to ask you if you don't mind?"

"It's not about…" Moira squeaked, looked at Ethan, who had appeared at Daisy's side and couldn't finish her question.

"It's about the shop. When it first opened. I thought you might be able to piece together a few things that are confusing me. But only if you don't mind?"

"Well, I'm not sure how we can be of any help, it's not either of our families that opened the shop, but perhaps we heard a few things."

"Well, that's just the thing, Lyle. Your relatives opened the shop with John's. It was in both their names."

"That can't be right. Can it Lyle? You have the wrong

information. My father's great grandparents opened the haberdashers. Lyle wasn't anything to do with the place until he met my father." Ethan looked between Daisy and Lyle, whose face was almost blank. No expression at all.

"That's correct son," There was that flash across Ethan's face again. "As far as I am aware, Daisy, John's family started the haberdashers and tailors alone."

"I have some original paperwork upstairs that shows that the Foster and Youngs set up the store together when the village was first being established."

At that moment, Moira's teacup clattered off the edge of her saucer, sending rivulets of Lady Grey across the tabletop. She let out a small cry, her hands fluttering up to cover her mouth.

"Come now, Moira, let's get you home; maybe this was a bit much for you after all." Lyle's hand was under her armpit and rising her out of her seat before Daisy had grabbed some serviettes and dabbed at the puddles. "Moira's having a bit of a bad day today, her nerves, you know" Lyle directed the words at Daisy but were loud enough for the whole shop, whose eyes were once again on them, then quieter added "About that family thing. Young isn't an unusual name; it must have been another family. Just a funny coincidence."

"Funny coincidence," Daisy repeated as the door banged closed with a clatter of the bell.

Confused about what had just happened, Daisy stayed sitting, watching the three figures cross the road and head up the steep, narrow path between the shops opposite. Halfway up they stopped; it seemed like strong words were being spoken. Lyle pointed at Ethan, who knocked away his hand and then seemed to plead with his mother, who stood quietly to one side. Ethan then stormed off down the lane between the backs of the shop gardens and the gardens of the houses above.

Mrs Puw, who had been making her way across the shop

filling up a tray with empties, began wiping up the tea and tutting at the wasted cakes, which hadn't even been touched.

"Should I ask?"

"I mean, you could. But I wouldn't have a clue how to answer you!" Daisy replied, still unsure of what exactly had just happened.

Chapter Fifteen

"Ah Inspector Locke, just the man I was hoping to meet."

Daisy approached the bench where DI Locke sat on the patch of grass by the police station steps. If it had been anyone else, Daisy would say that they were there enjoying the mid-morning sun. But the inspector looked anything but comfortable. His tie and top buttons were pulled loose revealing a large crucifix nestled amid some stray hairs. He mopped his face with a large white handkerchief as she sat down beside him.

"I've come to bring Dafydd Jones some lunch on behalf of the Valley Ladies Guild." She pulled aside the tea towel that covered two thermos flasks, bread and butter and some cakes. She frowned as the inspector shook his head.

"We feed him, he doesn't need any of that. I don't know what you're trying to do, but you are not allowed in to see him." Daisy smiled sweetly, she had been prepared just for this eventuality and pulled out a small book from the side of her basket.

"Actually, you don't have any choice but to let me in." She made a huge deal of flicking through the booklet, pausing as if to find the passage, even though she knew exactly the right page and even which paragraph she was aiming for. Finally, she tapped her finger on the third paragraph of page twenty seven titled WELFARE OF PRISONERS AT PENBODLEN POLICE STATION and began reading aloud.

"Following a committee meeting between the South Wales Constabulary, the Welsh Chapel, the Wesleyan Chapel, the Church in Wales and the local councillors, prisoners held at Penbodlen Police Station have a right to daily sustenance and moral guidance from the Valley Ladies Guild." She took a deep breath to continue, but he held out his hand and waved her away.

"Don't bother Miss Fields. I know these backwards little places have their own ways of doing things and I really couldn't care less. Go on. Have your little chat about morality and try to save the old codger's soul or whatever it is you want to do. Nothing you can say or do is going to help. He'll be off to the city in a few days and I can go back to my own desk, in my own office." The inspector mopped at the bead of sweat that ran down his left temple.

"Before you leave. I've been talking to some friends of mine at the Met about you Miss Fields."

"The Met, Inspector? I don't believe I know anyone at the Meteorological Office? Were you asking about the local weather specifically? David Davies over at Cefn Talcen farm is the best meteorologist around. All of the farmers know if David Davies is cutting his fields that they better get on and do it, even if they had other plans. He has never gotten it wrong and the locals haven't had a haylage crop spoil in decades."

Daisy took a deep breath wondering just how wide the man's eyes could get before he decided to stop her "Or do you mean The Metropolitan in town? The place where they do tea dances during the afternoons, but manage to draw the younger crowd in with live music of an evening? I hear they had a Death Metal weekend recently. Mrs Puw had quite the shock when she went to her hospital appointment let me tell you!"

"You know—" The inspector's voice squeaked and he cleared his throat before beginning at a much lower octave. "You are quite aware that I mean the Metropolitan Police Miss Fields. In London."

"Well one should speak clearly to ensure all parties understand the context Inspector. May I ask what it is you have discovered from your friends?" Daisy tried hard to keep her smile sweet.

"Well, nothing yet. Apparently I don't have the right clearance." Daisy stifled her sigh of relief by standing up quickly and ignoring his annoyance.

"I'm sure you'll learn anything you need to know if they decide it's at all relevant. Here have one of these biscuits." She wrapped a shortbread destined for the front desk in a serviette and placed it next to him on the bench.

Looking up at the imposing red brick building, the colour a stark contrast to the grey stone of the buildings surrounding it, she practically skipped up the steps and through into the cool of reception.

"Ah Tom, perfect." Daisy said as she placed the plate on the reception desk and slid it across to him. "Detective Inspector Locke has given his permission for me to visit with the prisoner."

"Has he now. Did he agree to this with an arm bent up behind his back?" Tom furrowed his eyebrows questioningly as he bit into a shortbread. Then rolled his eyes as she showed him the old, battered cover of the police booklet.

"What dusty shelf did you dig that thing off of? That's probably a hundred years old if it's a day! I bet you didn't mention what version we are on now." He said pulling a set of keys from beneath the desk and pressing the buzzer to open up the door.

"I don't know what you mean Sergeant. The Valley Ladies Guild still have the task of caring for prisoners written as part of our constitution so this must also be correct." She followed him past the offices which were a buzz of activity and understood why the inspector chose to sit out in the heat, even though it was much cooler inside. Daisy rubbed her arms against the chill of the corridor leading down to the four jail cells.

"Are you decent Daf? You have a visitor!" Tom called through the open flap in the door before pushing it open. Daisy could hear movement inside and a grunt as the unseen body of Dafydd Sparks shifted up to a sitting position.

"Decent? 'Tis bloody freezing in 'ere Tom. Another blanket I need, not a visitor."

"Now now, Daf, be polite. It's Daisy, Poppy's niece from the tea shop? She's the one who is going to help us get you out of this mess and she brought you something to eat to boot." Stepping back out of the tiny cell Tom left room for her to go inside.

"I'll leave the door ajar, if you could pull it to when you leave?" He whispered, leaning close enough she could feel the warmth of his breath on her cheek and smell the crisp, clean tone of his aftershave.

"Aren't you supposed to lock it?" She replied just as quietly, worried about being placed in charge of a prisoner.

"Yeah, but he ain't gonna do a runner with you here and I'll come back down and lock it when you've gone. Don't stress Daisy Chain he's just a big old puppy dog."

"Don't call me Daisy Chain." She said with a frown before plastering a smile on her face and walking inside. The cell, which was painted the same ice blue as the corridor, was just big enough for a narrow bed, which was more of a concrete bench with a mattress, and a metal toilet with a small basin built into the cistern.

"Dafydd, The Ladies Guild asked me to come and bring

you some food. Mrs Charles heard they only gave you microwave meals and came over all faint at the thought!"

The sight that beheld her was pitiful. In her knowledge of him Dafydd had always been a troubled man, each line in his face a scar of the trauma of losing his ability to care for his family and then losing his wife. but now? His eyes were drawn even more than usual, he looked positively gaunt.

The only benefit he seemed to have had was a shower and a change of clothes. Seeing him out of his tatty trousers and holey woolen jumpers beneath his long waxed overcoat and in a clean grey tracksuit was jarring.

"Mrs Charles said you were partial to her cawl so there is an extra large serving of that, plus some of Mr Brodbeck's white bloomer and she made sure it's thickly cut and spread generously with butter from the Hughes' dairy." She sat on the opposite end of the bed and placed the items of the basket onto a large napkin she'd spread between them. Dafydd didn't even wait for her to pour the contents of the thermos into the bowl. He pulled the top off and took a long deep breath.

"Aunty Pearl makes the best cawl. I've spent my entire life trying to guess exactly how she manages to make the lamb so tender. I've never managed it." He grabbed the spoon and savoured each and every mouthful. Daisy felt a little like she was the third wheel to this love affair between a man and his food. She took the opportunity to pour the hot water into the small travel teapot.

"Tom said you're going to get me out of all this mess?" Dafydd said between mouthfuls, his hand covering his mouth.

"Well, I'm trying to find out everything I can about the situation and see if there is anything I can do to help." She handed him a bottle of Mr Keppler's fiery ginger beer. "I'd like to ask you a few questions if you don't mind?" She said as he popped the lid and took a long hard drought. His face contorting as he swallowed the cold, spicy drink.

"Ooh, that hits the spot. Well, I can't refuse a kind young

thing who brings me all my favourite foods anything can I?" He rolled his hand at her as if telling her to continue, as he peeked inside each of the small containers.

"Okay then. We'd better get started, I'm not sure how long before Detective Inspector Locke will come and demand I leave." Pulling out her notepad, she flipped to the page where she had written some questions. Taking a sip of her tea she settled in to ask as many of them as she could manage.

"So, the night before you were arrested, it was Wednesday. Do you remember where you were and what you were doing before you went to sleep?"

"Of course I remember where I was. Farmer Boyce had given me some work for a week. I'd been sleeping in his barn loft and helping him rewire his cow barn electrics now the cows are out in the fields."

"Oh, I thought Tom said you helped with the sheep dipping?"

"Ah, well, yes I did a bit of everything. But I was mainly there to stop the barn being a fire hazard. I don't even want to imagine what would have happened if one of those wires caught. The whole place needed re-wiring top to bottom. All the wire insulation had been chewed by rats. There were even dead ones who'd electrocuted themselves. Poor buggers."

"Right, so you came back from the farm on Wednesday? What did you do after that?"

"I had some cash in my pocket so I went to the pub didn't I."

"Did you see John Foster at all?"

"Not that I know of." He said taking a bite of bread, the butter so thick it looked like a slice of cheese "Not that I really know the feller mind you. Never had much call for a suit beyond my funeral suit. Course Nelly would have known them. She was into all that. Always making new curtains, or clothes for herself and dresses for the new babies in the family." He looked at the thickly sliced bread as if the butter had soured right there in his hand. "She was never blessed with babies or the best of health was my Nelly. Sickly child she had been." He fell silent. Daisy gave him a moment, but didn't dare risk losing him to his melancholy.

"So you could have seen him and not known it was him?" She felt terrible for not comforting him in his distress, but she had obviously done the right thing as he sat up straighter and took another bite.

"I guess," He said around a mouthful of bread, this time not worrying about covering his mouth "but they've shown me a photo of him, and apart from some vague recollection of seeing him at a church get together one Christmas, I couldn't say."

"What time did you leave the pub?"

"Would have been chucking out time. Eleven thirty?"

"And you went straight to the park?"

"Couldn't really tell you to be honest. I was three sheets to the wind by that point wasn't I?"

"And you didn't see anyone at the park?"

"Look love, I don't even remember walking down and handing the police the knife. Let alone anything before I fell asleep." Daisy could feel the frustration in his voice and thought about the little bottle hidden in the bottom of the basket. She knew Dai wasn't an alcoholic, he only ever went to the pub on pay day when Nelly was alive and this was a habit he had kept since. But still, giving a man in custody a bottle of the thing that had gotten him into trouble in the first place made her uncomfortable.

"Perhaps this will help you bring back the memories?" She said quickly before she could back out. She reached under the tea towel in the bottom of the basket and retrieved the small bottle, tipping it into his empty cup so she could hide it again before anyone came in.

"What is it?" He took a sniff and nodded his head in acknowledgement before downing the drink in one. "You've done your homework." He stuck his nose into the cup, closed his eyes and breathed slowly and deeply.

Daisy had asked Eira, the pub landlady, what he had been drinking that night and had gratefully accepted the small taster bottle of a local whisky. She knew the smell would probably jolt his memory more than the amber coloured liquid itself.

She sat quietly while he breathed slowly and deeply. Then a small smile appeared on his face.

"It was a lovely clear night and I lay on a bench in the park to see the stars. I had originally planned on going up to the Camel's Hump but as I passed the park I remembered that Nelly loved to sit there when it was sunny." He took another deep breath and Daisy could see him battling with his grief.

"I must have dozed off, I was dreaming about the holiday in Devon where a goat tried to eat Nelly's hat." He chuckled at the memory, quickly replaced by a frown "I think there was a noise that disturbed me, pulling me out of the dream. Then, when I woke up there was something in my hand. The knife they said I stabbed that man with. I think there were footsteps running away."

He sank back against the wall and placed the cup in his lap. A single tear ran down his cheek.

"Oh Dafydd." She reached across and placed her hand on his. He took it and squeezed. More tears running down his face.

"To be honest, this is such a relief. I was beginning to question myself. That maybe I did kill him. How could I argue my innocence if I had no memories of the event in the first place?"

"Is there anything else you remember at all? Did you follow the footsteps?" Dafydd took another deep breath of the cup and spoke without opening his eyes "I did run down onto the street."

"And..."

"Someone was running away, I remember their footsteps

echoing as they ran up the valley. It was dark so I couldn't — a cape?" He cut himself off, his eyebrows narrowed in a quizzical expression "No...I think it was a long coat like mine? but darker, black maybe?"

"Did you see where they went?" He shook his head. "I called out and they just disappeared. I guess he must have ducked into a lane or a garden."

"And why did you come down to the shop? Why carry the murder weapon around with you?"

"I guess I saw the blue lights flashing and figured they were looking for the man. I was inebriated Daisy, I don't believe straight thinking is the drunkard's strong point. Do you?"

"No, I guess not" she chuckled, before her face dropped. A sense of shame enveloped her and the aching need to see this man freed overwhelmed her. She had known this man, if only from a distance, for years, appreciated his plight of losing both job and wife. But now, hearing him speak so eloquently, listening to the pain he had experienced in his life. She was ashamed to admit to herself that she had looked down on him. His dirty, ragged clothes. The way he'd always looked grubby. The way he wandered the streets and purposefully chose to sleep rough even though he had a perfectly pleasant home to live in. But worse, was the things other people said about him that had clouded her judgement.

A noise in the distance made her jump in the silence. She looked at her watch.

"I'd better go, I'll leave the containers and the rest of the ginger beer. Tom can give them back to me when you've finished with them." She began to clear away the tea things and the thermos flasks just as voices were heard at the end of the corridor. "I'll do whatever I can to help you Dafydd." She spoke quickly and with purpose "All your family and friends send their love. They believe, and are backing you every step of the way.

A fund has been set up in case it does go to court and Mrs

Charles's granddaughter Emily, has been in touch with her brother-in-law's uncle. He's some bigwig lawyer in London" she said verbatim "Someone from his office is coming to speak to you right as we speak because he is currently on another case, but he promises he will be here as soon as he is free."

The door banged open, a harassed looking DI Locke entered, followed by a young man in an expensive, tailored blue suit, carrying a large leather pouch.

"Dafydd, it seems you now have council." The inspector, with an aggrieved look on his face, gestured the man.

"I will see my client in a room with a table." He spoke with a strong Received Pronunciation accent and although he looked like he was barely out of short trousers, Daisy was impressed by his self assured nature. He hadn't asked for a different room. It was a demand. A demand he expected to be fulfilled.

"But…" The inspector spluttered. From the corridor Daisy could hear Tom speaking.

"Would the interview room suit your needs sir? It's about the best we can offer. We don't really have any space, particularly with all the extra staff."

"That will be grand. Thank you Sergeant." The young man nodded and then returned to face Dafydd. "Mr Jones, shall we go through?" He stood back and waited for Dafydd to leave, before he followed. Daisy could have sworn she saw him wink at someone out in the corridor.

Chapter Sixteen

Mrs Puw poured tea into the waiting cups while Michael leafed through some of the old diaries. Daisy was busy regaling them with the whole affair at the station. She had only stayed long enough to pack up her basket and straighten the bed, sweeping any crumbs off the wool blanket into her hand and flushing them down the toilet.

That toilet having a huge effect on her resolve to help Dafydd get released as quickly as possible. It's not that it was smelly or dirty, in fact it was pristine, with a hint of pine fresh cleaner, but knowing that he was effectively sleeping in a bathroom made her shudder.

"I didn't think the inspector's face could have got any redder when I saw him on the bench outside the station. But when I left, he was practically grey. I don't think this case is agreeing with his health at all."

"So young Billy had no issues seeing Dafydd?" Mrs Puw asked, pushing a plate of Welsh cakes into the centre of the table and handing them each a cup.

"Oh, you should have seen him, Mrs Puw. He walked and talked as if he owned the place." She thought about the wink. "Do Tom and Billy know each other then?"

"Oh yes, love, they are cousins. Their grandmothers are sisters. Billy's was in service at that big manor house that's a hotel now, Plas Treowen, until the family upped and went back to London and she jumped at the chance to leave with them. Always had big dreams, that one. She became lady's maid to one of the daughters." Mrs Puw gave off an air of triumph as she spoke, as if this position held the highest regard in the world. Daisy figured that to someone who had grown up in this tiny village and suffered through strikes and abject poverty at various points in her life, it probably was.

"And it's lucky she did or she would never have met my grandfather and I wouldn't be here to save the day."

They all spun round to see Tom and Billy standing in the doorway. Billy's accent had softened into a broader London twang, and he looked far less standoffish with his tie loosened, his top buttons undone and his jacket thrown over one shoulder.

"Oh, Billy, how lovely to see you. Come on, come and give me a big cwtch." Billy moved around the table in two long strides and embraced Mrs Puw before giving her a large peck on the cheek. Michael and Daisy both raised their eyebrows at the sight, not used to seeing the usually stoic Mrs Puw being so affectionate.

"Lovely to see you too, Aunty Olwen. I can't wait for you to come back and visit this summer. There's a new exhibition I'm dying to take you to."

"Oh, bachgen da." Mrs Puw patted his cheek and tilted her head as she looked at him affectionately. "Nawr te. You two sit; I want to hear all about it." She beckoned to the newcomers. Billy grabbed the back of Tom's usual chair by the back door, but Tom gave him a friendly shove to the chair next to Michael, gaining himself a disapproving swat of the tea towel from Mrs Puw.

"Sadly, we don't have enough to get Mr Jones released now this minute." All four of them had listened intently to

Billy for ten solid minutes as he ran through everything Dafydd had told him. There were a few small things he had remembered after Daisy had left, but nothing of major importance. "But there have been so many errors in following protocol, or simply errors, like them searching the wrong park." He shook his head as he said this. "That Mr Eisenberg says the case will get thrown out of court if it even gets that far. Not that he thinks it will." They all sat silently for a few minutes, Daisy ruminating on everything she had learnt that day. And there was so much information to run through.

"So, I'm confused." Michael broke the silence.

"Well, that's not an unusual state of affairs, is it?" Tom laughed and nudged Michael in the arm.

"Oh haha. So, Mr Eisenberg is somebody's granddaughter's brother-in-law's something or other? So, nothing to do with this valley, right?"

"Right." They all said in unison.

"So...how did you get a job there? That's one hell of a coinkydink, isn't it? That this bigwig lawyer and Billy here both have ties to the valley yet live hundreds of miles away?"

"Firstly," said Tom halfway through eating a Welsh cake, "never say that word in my presence again."

"Second," continued Billy, "Nanny Mildred never really left the valley. She might have had itchy feet to see the world, but she stayed as connected as she could possibly be. She spoke to family members on the phone every Friday and wrote letters every single day of the week to various people. By hand, would never dream of writing a text or an email.

"When she found out I wanted to be a lawyer, the first thing she did was write to her old friends. I know it seems like an insular little place. But out there? The tendrils of this valley reach far and wide. I have an offer from someone's distant relative to work in Canada if I ever wanted to. But Mr Eisenberg's offices were an hour's bus ride from my house. He offered me work experience during the school holidays. It was supposed to be travel expenses only that first summer holiday, but he must have liked what he saw. He got me a full scholarship to a private sixth form college and helped me with my interviews for uni. In all honesty, I owe everything to him."

"Nonsense," Mrs Puw cut in. "You got yourself that scholarship, and your place at university. Just because he spoke to a few people to get you into the exam doesn't negate all the hard work you did by passing." Mrs Puw rose without speaking further and began fussing with the casserole. Billy grimaced, afraid he'd upset her. Daisy shook her head and patted his hand, reassuring him he was good.

"What I want to know is why Billy boy calls you Aunty Olwen and I call you Mrs Puw?" Tom acted offended.

"That's because Billy's grandmother and I were firm friends at school, and I visited with her every chance I was able."

"But Great Aunt Mildred passed away four years ago?"

"And? Should I stop visiting with people who I class as friends and family just because one of them is dead, Tomos Griffith?"

"Of course not, Mrs Puw." Tom spoke with a mumble and looked down into his cup.

"Besides, Billy and I have the same tastes in art, and we enjoy visiting the galleries when I'm in town." Mrs Puw calling London 'town,' amused Daisy greatly, and she had to cover a chortle with a cough.

This was enough to bring Tom out of his reverie, and he looked at Daisy with an amused expression on his face, mouthing, 'art?' at her. She frowned at him, but couldn't quite hide her own smirk.

"Anyway. Hisht nawr Tom, I want Billy to tell me all about this new exhibition while we eat our tea."

Chapter Seventeen

Thursday morning and the babbling giggles of six toddlers as they played in the children's corner filled the tea shop. Daisy stopped wiping down a table to watch her youngest regulars, who had been coming since they were babes in arms.

"Daidy, Daidy." The quiet singsong voice brought her attention to the small boy tugging at her trouser leg, his hand leaving a damp patch from where he had been chewing his fingers.

"Hello Macsen, why aren't you playing with your friends?" She crouched down, so that she was at his level.

"Biccet?" he asked, nodding his head so enthusiastically his blonde curls bobbed wildly.

"Yes, your biccet, I mean biscuits, and juice will be coming out any minute."

His dribbly grin showed off his bright white teeth, and he toddled back to his mother shouting, "Dws, dws, dws," at the top of his voice. Daisy laughed at the smiling tractor on the bum of the brightly striped leggings. Macsen's father being a farmer made it all the funnier.

"Daisy." Another hand grabbed at hers. This time it was an adult hand and much drier that little Macsen's. "I haven't forgotten that I need to pay you. I'll come over in a bit when Freddie is done." Sylvia was nursing baby Freddie, who was trying to poke his fingers up her nose.

"Don't worry, I know where you live," Daisy said laughing, patting the young woman's hand. "Did the teething biscuits help?"

"Oh, so much. I might need some more from you soon; the box in the freezer is practically empty."

"Well, you'll be here a couple of hours, I'll get Michael to whip up a batch, he's been pestering me to give him Aunty Poppy's secret recipe for years."

"Did I hear you were making those wonderful teething biscuits?" Asked Maisy Donelly, the mother of two sets of twins, Daisy remembered making the teethers for Alys and Beca, who were now in school "I've been so tired, I completely forgot how wonderful they were for the girls."

"Those boys aren't getting teeth already, are they?" Daisy exclaimed, peering into the pram at the two tiny babies wrapped in coordinating blue and purple blankets "They are still so small. I swear they were only born yesterday."

"Rhys has started gnawing on his hands, and I can already see some white dots on Osian's gums."

"Any chance we can get some chunkier ones, Daisy? Macsen has some molars coming in, but I think he'd chomp right through the baby ones."

"Don't worry, mammies, I'll make sure there are plenty ready for you all to take some home with you to keep for emergencies. Even if they aren't needed yet." Michael said as he appeared at her side with a tray of biscuits and a large jug of apple juice, that was more water than juice.

"Here you go, ladies and gentlemen. Drinks and biccies for everyone." He said to the children, who all ran over to collect the gingerbread men that were almost as big as their faces. Raisins marking the eyes and buttons.

"Michael, wrap up two for Maisy's girls. They can have

them on the way home from school if that's okay?" Daisy said before turning back to the group, "We'll bring your teas out in just a moment."

The bell above the door rang and Daisy turned expecting to welcome some tourists looking for a sit down and a nice cuppa. Instead she was surprised to find Ethan Foster weaving his way through the tables, most of which were empty and sitting himself at the one closest to the end of the display cabinet.

"I'll leave this with you?" She asked Michael, who smiled, nodded and continued to talk to the group.

"Ethan, I wasn't expecting to see you today." She said as she neared, drawing his attention away from something down by his foot. "Thursday mornings are always a bit frantic, so locals tend to stay away." This drew a shake of the head and tuts from a middle-aged couple obviously intent on hitting the mountain trail in their brand new walking gear.

"Oh, that's fine; they are only children." He sat up straight, pulling his feet under his seat. "Look, I'm sorry about my mother. She can be a bit nervy at the best of times, but this last week she's been so on edge. I think him coming back has brought up all the old feelings, you know?" He practically spat the word him, a glimmer of disgust on his face.

"Of course, it must have been a shock to the system. What can I get you?"

"Just a cuppa, please."

"You not working today?" Daisy asked, returning a few moments later with his pot of tea and a caramel chocolate finger.

"I've taken some time off work. I think things have got to me a bit, but Hannah was mopping the floors and told me to get out of the house for an hour or two." Daisy had seen this many times before with the newly retired men in the community. Sent out of the house to do some chore or another, or because the floor suddenly needed mopping or hoovering when in fact it was merely the wives needing to get their spouses, although much loved, out from under their feet.

"Before you go, Daisy." He placed his hand firmly on her wrist as she turned to leave before quickly removing it again. "Erm. You said something about paperwork you had upstairs in your flat? About the old shop?"

"Yes, that's right. I haven't been through it all yet; there's so much of it. But there's a lot of interesting things."

"And there's stuff about my dad?"

"It's all from a very long time ago, I think. But like I said, I haven't finished. You're more than welcome to come and have a look at the flat sometime. It's where your great grandparents lived; you can look through the papers as well? They are mentioned in there."

"Maybe I will. It'll be nice to see where my grandparents lived. Thanks" He reached across to the next table and grabbed the week's local paper from a pile. "Might as well catch up on what's going on around here." And he disappeared behind the newspaper.

"Leaving so early, Sylvia?" Daisy said an hour later, the rest of the mother's group still sitting around enjoying the peace as the toddlers played. "The teething biscuits aren't quite ready yet."

"Oh no, I just wanted to pay you while Freddie was sleeping. He's going through a bit of a separation anxiety phase at the moment. Card okay?" She waved her phone at Daisy, who went behind the counter to find the little white card reader that had been buried under a pile of paper bags.

"How did the tarte tatin go down? Did Peter's mother enjoy the meal?" Daisy fiddled with the box, pressing the buttons hard trying to get it to work. "Confounded thing," she muttered under her breath as she added too many zeros and had to start again.

"Oh, it was delicious. She even took a slice home with her along with some of the lamb I cooked and said she was going to have it for her lunch the next day! I almost fell over when she said it. I offer leftovers every time, and she's always politely declined."

"Well, that's a turnaround for the books!"

"I think she felt sorry for me, Freddie whimpered the entire time she was there. Apparently, Peter suffered terribly every time he was teething, and she didn't sleep for a week when he got his first tooth."

"Are you still having to walk the streets at night with him?"

"Not for the last few days, I think we are over the worst with this tooth. I'm hoping for a bit of a break before the next one!" She pushed her phone into her back pocket.

"Was that Ethan Foster that was here?" Daisy looked across and noticed that his table was indeed empty.

"Yes, he's having a few days off, by the sounds of it. Must be nice for Hannah to have him home. I think he was away with his work last week."

"No, that can't be right. I saw them both a couple of times last week with all my comings and goings with the young Mr Grumpy Bum over there." She inclined her head towards the sofas.

"Are you sure, Sylvia? Can you recall what days it was you saw him?"

A wail came from the sofas and a call of Sylvia's name.

"I don't know off the top of my head, sorry. I'll have a think though, yeah?"

"If you could, just call me anytime if you aren't passing." She held Sylvia's hand as she handed her the receipt. "It could be really important."

"Droopy Drawers, forty-four."

"House. House." Came a shout from the back of the room, which filled with chatter while the numbers were checked.

"Thanks for inviting me out, Mrs Puw. This is actually quite fun!" Daisy looked down at the pitiful attempt on her bingo cards. Mrs Puw and Mrs Roberts both having three full books in front of them and a row of coloured dabbers standing on end.

"You needed to get out of that flat. You've been stuck up there every evening with those old books. Have you even spent time on your allotment this week?" She opened her mouth and closed it again knowing that she was only asking because Bill Thumb, whose surname was actually White but had always had a green thumb, would have already told her he'd been watering Daisy's plot as she hadn't been there.

She simply shook her head and took a sip of her drink.

"Before I forget. We'll need to get a man round to fix the bottom of the display unit. It looks like there's a loose plank at the end. It was practically hanging off when I moved the table back to its right spot earlier."

"Kids, I expect. They like to lean against that side of the display; it's warm from the cooling unit." Daisy made a mental note to check it out as the bingo caller, a grey-haired man in a blue velour jacket, brought everyone back to attention. Mrs Puw had always "got a man in", usually Billy Bits the local handyman, but Daisy preferred to fix things herself where she could. She had managed her own flat in London for years after her parents passed away and tried her hardest to fix anything she could before resorting to paying for it.

Daisy's head was filled with bingofied numbers as she wandered home at the end of the night. The workingmen's club was just at the top of Commercial Street and around the corner up the hill. She wandered down the middle of the road enjoying the light breeze on the cool night air, the sound of a car in the distance made her change her mind and instead of walking the whole way down the street she turned left and into the lane that ran the whole length of the back of the street.

In the darkness, the river gurgled and sloshed over the sounds of her footsteps. The birds had gone to sleep hours ago, but the crickets still chirruped amongst the cooling grass, and bats swooped against the starry night. The only light from the buildings was the kitchen light from the flat above the post office. Moths fluttered against the bright window, and the shadows shortened as she neared.

Stepping through the beam of light, everything seemed suddenly darker on the other side. The river rushed faster, and the sound of her footsteps echoed back to her.

Wait. That wasn't the echo of her own footsteps.

Footsteps grew louder as they ran towards her.

She peered into the darkness, wishing the light from the window hadn't destroyed her night vision.

"Hello? Who's that?" She called, stepping back.

But the footsteps kept coming at her. Picking up speed until the figure pushed past, knocking her to the ground with a grunt.

"Bloody kids." She muttered, wondering which of the valley's teenage boys she'd just caught up to no good. "Ouch." She rubbed her left hip as she dragged herself back up to her feet and dusted herself down. Each step hurting more than the last as she slowly made her way up the lane.

She leant heavily on the wall as she carefully made her way up her steps, grateful to almost be at her bed.

But as soon as she came to her door, she knew her bed would lie cold for a while longer yet.

Chapter Eighteen

"Do you think anything is missing?" Tom asked, giving her a cup of tea. Daisy was on her sofa, with a pillow under her knees and a hot water bottle against her hip. She shifted to sit up straighter and winced at the pain shooting down her leg.

"I don't know Tom. I don't think so, but there are papers everywhere. Like they've been thrown in the air."

"And you're sure it was a teenager who ran past you?"

"It could have been an adult. But not a very large man. It definitely wasn't Lyle if that's where you're going. They had their hood pulled over their face."

It had been barely twenty minutes since she had reached inside her back door to turn on the light and seeing the mess inside. It had taken Tom less than 5 minutes to get the entire night shift, of which there were four officers, into a squad car and at her door, blue lights blazing.

She had been mortified and had made him know exactly as much.

"It's not an emergency, is it, Tom?" She had hissed between her teeth so his officers didn't hear. "Did you really have to bring the entire village out to my door? Again? Three times in one week!"

"There could have been someone still inside Daisy." He had hissed back between grinning teeth as he helped her into the back seat of the car to sit while they finished checking for damage.

"You called the doctor?" She said, as Dr Silwa strode through the arch in his dressing gown and carrying his medical bag.

"You're lucky I didn't call an ambulance; you said you were hurt."

Nestled on her sofa, she felt quite angry, not at Tom's reaction, or the embarrassment at the whole situation. But at the reasoning someone would have had for breaking into her flat. She knew she had left her door unlocked accidentally in the past, something she'd never have done in London. Had she left it ajar enticing some ruffian in who had nothing better to do with their evening? She had nothing of value. Is that why they threw all the papers and books everywhere? Why they had swiped across the work surfaces and knocked everything to the ground?

"Oh, no." She sighed

"What? What is it? Is everything alright?" Tom was at her side in a second, looking her over, his face grave with worry. "Shall I get Silwa back?"

"What? No I'm fine Tom," she said swatting him away, "what if they've damaged Marianne's diaries? I promised I would keep those safe for the family. I need to go and pick them all up carefully."

"No, you don't. I'll get the town constables to do that when they've finished dusting for prints. I'll make sure they leave the place a damn sight better than they left the shop, don't you worry about that. Now drink your tea and take those painkillers the doc gave you for yer bum."

"It's my hip, Tom."

"Course it is." He laughed and disappeared into the kitchen, pulling the door closed behind him. She could hear him giving orders to be careful and asking if they really thought the thieves would have gone in the fridge? Barnaby jumped up and nestled on her lap, his head resting on the hot water bottle.

"I moved here for a quiet life, Barnaby. What happened to that, huh?" The ginger cat mewled his reply, "Why does this village seem to have it in for me this week?" Then she felt bad. A man had lost his life, she couldn't really think it was all about her. "Well, not me. But our little shop at the very least." She laid her head back and hoped the police would be out of her hair soon. She really was so tired, she closed her eyes just for a moment.

Friday morning, Daisy awoke in her bed, fully clothed. Her head felt heavy and woozy as she tried to sit up. She grabbed for her glasses, but still not everything came back into focus.

"Ooh," she moaned as a searing pain jolted through her left side. She felt like she'd been hit by a bus.

"I thought I heard you." Mrs Puw came bustling into her bedroom with a tray in her hands. "Now you're to stay in bed at least until the doctor comes back later this afternoon." She placed the tray on Daisy's lap after she had managed to wiggle herself into a sitting position without too much pain.

"I can't stay in bed, Mrs Puw. I have things to do, a shop to run."

"You'll do as you're told or I'll tell the doctor you need to go to hospital."

"You wouldn't?" But Daisy knew she would and slumped back into her pillow. "Why do I feel so groggy?"

"The doctor gave you some powerful painkillers. Thought they'd do you some good, what with the shock and the pain in your bottom." The last word she mouthed silently, inclining her head towards Daisy's middle with raised eyebrows as if it were a taboo word.

"It's my hip, no matter what Tom told you!" Daisy groaned, knowing that her backside would likely be the talk of the whole village by now.

"Same horse, different jockey." Mrs Puw said, pulling open the curtains to reveal a bright blue sky beyond. "Now eat; I need to get back down to the shop."

"The shop! Who's looking after the shop?"

"Stop fretting, will you? Billy has been helping me, and Tom said he'll be in after he's had some sleep. Oh, I almost forgot." She said, raising her finger in a silent 'wait here' as if Daisy was going anywhere. She disappeared through the bedroom door and returned with a hot water bottle. "Here, I thought you might want a fresh one for your..." She waggled her finger towards Daisy's lap, obviously saying the word once was too much for her and she couldn't even bring herself to say it again.

"It's my hip, Mrs Puw. My hip. Not my bum, or my bottom, or my pen ôl, or whatever else you don't want to call it. My hip!" said Daisy, slipping the fluffy hot bottle down her side. The heat felt good.

"Oh, Daisy, don't talk mucky now." Mrs Puw said as she smoothed the duvet back down over Daisy's legs and picked off imaginary bits of fluff in her awkwardness. Daisy often wondered how ladies of a certain generation managed to tell the doctor about any intimate issues. "Now you get on and eat before that gets cold."

Left alone, the smell of the freshly toasted bread suddenly made her ravenous. She devoured the toast with homemade raspberry jam and tucked in to the bowl of porridge with sliced banana and an extra generous sprinkling of brown sugar. The small glass of orange juice that Mrs Puw believed was obligatory to drink every morning made her laugh, but the small mouthful finished her breakfast off perfectly. Hunger satiated, she relaxed to drink her tea, English Breakfast, the best way to start a morning.

It took less than an hour of staring at the sky and rooftops beyond the net curtains, at the wall, at the little bobbly bits on the duvet cover before Daisy was driving herself round the bend. After carefully manoeuvring herself off the bed she waddled carefully into her kitchen, each step sending a deep shooting pain up through her left hip and down her thigh.

"I thought you were told to stay in bed until I arrived, young lady." Dr Silwa said as he walked through the kitchen door at the very same second. Instead of his dressing gown, he was now fully dressed, in his usual tweed suit, bag still in hand.

"I, erm..." Daisy was so tired she struggled to think of an excuse quickly enough, but the doctor just chuckled.

"Don't worry, I won't tell on you." He nodded his head towards the tea shop downstairs. "At least lay back down long enough for me to check you over so I don't get a row either. That Olwen Michaels, as was, always had a way about her. Did you know she became head girl because she told the headmaster she was unimpressed with how he ran the school and she was going to whip it into shape? She did too! Always thought she should have gone into politics myself."

Ten minutes and a prescription for some less potent painkillers later, Doctor Silwa left, giving her a stern instruction to take it easy with a warning that it was mostly just going to 'hurt like the Dickens' for a few days.

By the time Mrs Puw came back upstairs Daisy was sat in the middle of her living room on the comfiest cushion she owned, being glared at from afar by Barnaby who usually took his morning nap on the very cushion, and was deep into the box of paperwork trying to find some semblance of order.

"Nefi Blw. Look at the mess!" Mrs Puw threw her arms up with an air of desperation and turned back into the kitchen, calling back, "Come and eat some dinner, will you? At least pretend to do as you're told?"

Gripping onto the arms of the chair, Daisy gritted her teeth and pulled herself up with a grunt, in such an undignified manner she was grateful Barnaby couldn't talk. She was stiff and aching, but was up on her feet and lying to herself that she was just fine.

"Sit, eat," Mrs Puw ordered her while she poured boiling water over the tea leaves in the waiting pot. "While you eat your soup, carrot and lentil, which that young slip of a thing that calls herself a 'soup witch' brought by. She heard about your little fall and said it's full of healing herbs or some such thing."

"Willow came round? You should have sent her up." Daisy ate a spoonful of the herby, spicy soup, the hot, thick liquid warming her from inside.

"She just popped in with the pot of soup; she had to get back before the dinnertime rush. It is midday, you know." Mrs Puw placed a glass of water and the packet of painkillers next to her. "Talking of, I have to get back downstairs before those boys destroy the place."

"Can you send Tom up when it's quiet again? I have some things he might need to know about Lyle's family."

Mrs Puw tutted as she left. "Never bloody stops, that one," Daisy heard as the door closed.

"She's a fine one to talk," Daisy said to Barnaby, who was sitting opposite her, his chin resting on the table as he watched the crusty bread roll in her hand, "no people food for cats in this house." She said, dipping a piece in her bowl and popping it in her mouth.

Barnaby let out a quiet, soulful meow and wiped at his whiskers with his paw, never taking his eyes off her.

"Okay. One tiny piece if you stop watching me." She tore off a small chunk of the still warm, golden brown crust and held it while Barnaby gently took it between his teeth, did a funny little flick of his head to get it into his mouth and crunched away happily.

Chapter Nineteen

Anyone driving past the police station that Saturday morning would have been forgiven for thinking that there was a community fete being held on the green across the road. By midday, the triangle of grass was barely visible for the blankets filled with families eating picnics. There were trestle tables manned by the Ladies Guild full of cups, huge steel teapots and thermos jugs that had been brought across from the village hall. Plates filled with refreshments kept appearing as fast as the empty ones had been cleared away.

Ben Bystander, who got his name by always seeming to find himself near trouble but never actually being involved, turned up with his band, The Pitmen. The lively folk music filled the valley as people danced in the cleared area of grass in front of their makeshift stage. The side of their van open to reveal the drummer centred between two stacks of speakers.

Ordered to sit in a well-padded lawn chair, Daisy tapped her foot to the lively music. It always surprised her how quickly a get together could happen here. All this had started with some of Dafydd's closest friends and family learning that Mr Eisenberg was finally coming to meet with him that morning. They had gathered to await his arrival, nervous for Dafydd's future and wanting to be there as support, even if it was from across the street.

By the time the well-dressed lawyer had arrived, Tom had to hold people back from trying to help him open his car door. Mr Eisenberg's hand had been shaken multiple times, and he had to ask people to stop trying to give him envelopes of cash.

"You might want to come with me so you can get a good view." Daisy jumped as Tom's breath tickled her ear.

"Why do you insist on creeping up on me?" Daisy said, her hand over her racing heart. "What do you mean a good view?"

"Come on, you'll soon find out." He held her hand as she stood stiffly. "Quick as you can; you don't want to miss this." With his hand on her back, Tom led her through the crowd, which diligently opened before her like the parting of the Red Sea. He left her stood on the edge of the police station steps just as the doors flung open.

The gathering fell into silence, the dying notes of a fiddle the last sound to be heard as Mr Eisenberg stepped out into the sunshine. He had a grave look on his face, and the villagers held a collective breath waiting for him to speak.

He cleared his throat, but didn't say a word, only stepped to one side and looked back into the doorway.

The silence erupted into cheers and cries as Dafydd, dressed in yet another tracksuit, this time a very fetching burgundy, stepped out of the police station door. The crowd moved as one across the road and in seconds, the man and his lawyer were surrounded. More hands were offered. More envelopes of money pushed towards the lawyer, and Dafydd's back received more claps than he'd received in his life.

Cars that had been travelling past had been deserted on the road, the drivers all joining in the celebrations.

Dafydd, who had been passed around all the women to be hugged and petted, finally made his way back up to the top step and held his hands up. Silence fell once more.

"I don't really know what to say. Thank you, to everyone who has helped me and stood by me." He said, his awkwardness showing in the way he wrung his hands, the toe of his right foot grinding into the stone beneath his feet. Daisy understood how difficult this must be for a man who had essentially lived as a hermit for the last few decades. "Mr Eisenberg? Where are you?" Hand shielding his eyes, he peered at all the faces until he found the one he had been looking for. "Come on lads, let him back up here, yeah?" Looking much more tousled than when he arrived, Mr Eisenberg made his way back up beside his client.

"Thank you." He whispered to Dafydd as he straightened his tie. He smiled as he turned to face the crowd. When he spoke again, it was exactly as Daisy had expected him to sound. Well-mannered and as if he had stepped out of a law show on the telly.

"Thank you, everyone. You will all be pleased to know that justice has prevailed here today in Penbodlen. After learning of the manner your family member and friend, Dafydd Jones, had been detained, the lack of evidence and poor justification behind his arrest, I am happy to say that all charges have been dropped. Dafydd will no longer be held by the police, and I will be seeking a written apology and monetary recompense for the serious misconduct that led to his being held for so long."

The crowd cheered again, and the two figures disappeared in the throng of people as they all decamped back to the green. The music started up, and Daisy, who had kept out of the crowd, watched as the real party began. She sat on the stone step and watched, her heart soaring for the man who was no longer facing life behind bars and was free to wander the hills and mountains once again.

"You know you did that?" Tom said, sitting next to her, pointing across to the party, the band had started back up, and alcoholic drinks were rapidly replacing the cups and saucers on the trestle tables.

"Nah, that was all Mrs Puw and Mr Eisenberg's doing." She said, her elbows on her knees, her chin resting on her fists.

"No, I mean it." Tom insisted, "If you hadn't have gone looking and found that blood, there would have been no physical proof the town lot had searched the wrong park. It could all have been explained away as an admin error without that, and Daf would have been carted off this afternoon."

"I thought they were supposed to have moved him on Wednesday? What happened there?" She said, frowning at the mischievous smirk that appeared on Tom's face. "What did you do, Tom?"

"Me?" he said with an air of humorous indignation, his hand on his chest. "Why would you think I did anything?"

"Tomos Griffith. You were supposed to be keeping your nose clean so nothing could be traced back to you! That's why I was the one doing the searching, remember?"

"Come on now, Daisy Chain, listen."

"Don't call me Daisy Chain." Daisy folded her arms across her chest and shook her head at him judgementally.

"I swear I didn't do anything wrong…" He chewed his lip. "It's not my fault it was left to a junior officer to fill in the transfer requisition form. It's also not my fault that the junior officer hasn't had the appropriate training with the new forms and accidentally filled in the old form that is missing some of the new mandatory information needed, making the transfer void."

He blew out his cheeks, letting the air out of his pursed lips slowly. "And it definitely is not my fault that all this was revealed too late on Wednesday to get the correct forms in place on Thursday for the transfer to happen on Friday. Then of course a special request needed to be made for a vehicle for a weekend transfer." He shook his head glumly. "All this paperwork and bureaucracy are making this job so difficult."

"Oh Tom. You, Mickey and Duncan need to be really careful. You don't want any of your jobs put in jeopardy."

Tom opened his mouth to reply, but the bang of the inner door hitting the wall drove him quickly to his feet.

"Sergeant. Get your backside in here and do the job you're being paid for." The detective inspector's voice seems strained as if he were trying, and failing, not to shout, "Unless you want to join the party? Then you can get in the unemployment line on Monday morning." The door banged shut.

"I'd better go and sort out all this paperwork. Don't want Mickey doing it and finding himself being investigated or on probation or anything. See you later, Daisy Chain. You go enjoy the festivities. I'm sure they will still be going at 6pm when I get off."

Moving to the bench she had sat on with DI Locke; Daisy quietly watched the crowd. Her eyes landed on face after face. Ones she knew intimately, others she knew to say hello to, some she only knew from afar. But each one was there for Dafydd. Was the real murderer among the revellers? Were they celebrating Dafydd's release after being the ones to get him arrested in the first place?

"They certainly are a lively lot, aren't they!" Mr Eisenberg sat by her side, a still full glass of beer in his hand.

"Oh yes, they put up a good party that's for sure." She turned to face the elderly lawyer and stuck out her hand. "Thank you so much for coming all this way. I'm not sure who has what over you, but you really pulled it out of the bag to help Dafydd. Well, this community as a whole, really."

"Miss Fields, I'm very used to the pull this little valley has on people. I'm only very distantly related, but even I have felt the lure of these mountains since I first visited. For a wedding. Then we came for a christening or two, and I had to admit I was hooked."

"I get that. I used to visit with my aunt when I was a child."

"Oh, I know all about you, Daisy. I was Poppy's solicitor for many years. I helped her put together her will and arranged for the shop to be transferred to you when you were still knee high to a grasshopper." He held out his hand about two feet off the floor. "About this big the last time you met me. But I've been following your life since then."

"What do you mean?" An icy shiver ran down Daisy's spine. Why was this man, who was a stranger to her, watching her?

"Don't fret, my dear. It's not as ominous as I made it sound." He said with a small laugh as he leant over and patted her hand. "Poppy asked me to keep an eye out for you. She never liked that you chose to stay in London after all that trouble and was worried about you. But our jobs kept us both in similar, if not distant, circles."

"Daisy, Mammy said to come and get some cake! You too, mister." The call came from a young boy, who disappeared back into the crowd before Daisy could even see his face.

"Well, it looks like our peace and quiet has come to an end. Don't look so concerned Daisy, I wasn't keeping tabs on you and reporting back to your aunt or anything. I just kept half an eye on your work, which was easy. The clients of the Victim and Witness Services and the Law tend to cross over all the time, don't they!"

"Mr Eisenberg, come and cut the cake!" A voice called from amid the crowd.

"You know, I really do like this place. One day soon I think I'll retire from the city. The thrill has gone for me after all these years. I might even open a little office in town just to keep my hand in, you know?" He stood and offered his free hand to Daisy, his other still nursing his full beer. She took it, unsure what to make of this man, who knew far more about her than she knew about him. Gritting her teeth as she eased past the stiffness in her hip, she stood, and they walked across the road together arm in arm.

Mr Eisenberg disappeared into the crowd to cheers and singing. Daisy stayed at the edge, not wanting to be jostled.

A flash of light caught her eye. Looking around for the source, she peered between the houses on the hill. There it was again. Another flash of light, as if the sun were catching on a reflective surface.

Peering past the glare, Daisy saw the outline of a dark figure.

And then they were gone.

Chapter Twenty

The party had gone on well into the night. At sunset, the younger partygoers were collectively shuffled off home to bed by their mothers, full of fizzy drinks, hot dogs, burgers, and cakes. The barbecue having arrived late in the afternoon in the butcher's van. The sleepy children with smudged face paints adamant that they weren't tired, despite the yawns, that they wanted to go to the pub with their daddies!

Daisy had taken the opportunity to sneak off home as the crowd dispersed, the women and children off up the hills to home; the rugby, football and cricket boys to their respective clubs, leaving a trail of mostly the over fifties, Dafydd Spark included, to the pub. Mr Eisenberg was nowhere to be seen, and Daisy suspected he had slipped off unnoticed many hours earlier.

Laying in bed with a cuppa and the next in the series of Marianne's diaries, Daisy couldn't wait for the next day.

Sunday.

No alarm to wake her at an ungodly hour. No hours of baking and preparation before the shop even opens. No day in the shop with the social meter set too high as people came and went all day.

Of course, Daisy loved the tea shop. It was the best job she had ever had. She loved the people and the tea and the baking.

But she loved a lie in too.

Sunday morning Daisy awoke feeling refreshed, having not been disturbed all night, a rare event in recent days. In her usual Sunday morning tradition, she brought tea and toast into bed to read until the pot was empty. But today Daisy couldn't focus on the words, her thoughts drifting to Dafydd's arrest and, thankfully, his release. Mr Eisenberg's cryptic comments about keeping an eye on her and even thinking about the figure at the top of the hill. Who was that staring down at the festivities?

She'd read the same first paragraph of Marianne's next entry three times without even realising until she took a bite of toast, wiped her fingers on the tea towel and tried to find her spot again.

"Come on, Daisy, let's at least finish this page before giving up, yeah?" She said to herself sternly, going back to the beginning and finally reading about the rumours going around amongst the shopkeepers that one shop was already looking like they were going to fail before the doors even opened.

Daisy's interest piqued, and she avidly flicked through the next three entries hoping there would be more detail about the issues. But there was nothing except Marianne's fawning over a certain young miner who had caught her eye. As analytical and exact as Marianne's diaries were, she was still a young girl, and young boys caught young girl's eyes.

Sundays were also clean sheets day. No matter how much she loved breakfast in bed, she hated the inevitable crumbs worse. She readied herself for her usual battle with the duvet cover, and although she still ended up in a sweaty mess, she avoided getting herself in a knot, or finding herself inside the cover instead of the actual duvet.

Freshly showered and wearing her snazzy Sunday best, which included a pair of purple joggers with a hole in the knee and her favourite, well-worn t-shirt, the one with the picture of a teacup sitting on an open book, the words Read it and Steep formed in the steam. Daisy wondered what to do with the rest of her day. She could take a small stroll? Her hip did seem much better now. Watch a film on the telly?

"Actually, you know what we are going to do today, Barnaby? We are going to get ahead of the week." Pulling on her purple cardigan and wrapping it tightly around her. She pushed her feet into her slippers and headed down to the kitchen.

Daisy placed the chair against the open kitchen door, allowing the breeze to get some fresh air inside. Inventory was something Daisy usually did in a rush on a Monday morning just as the shop opened. Doing it today meant that the order for the wholesalers would be done and sent over ready.

Daisy hummed as she worked. Counting off the items in each cupboard and on every shelf. Measuring the contents of the jars and adding to her list the things that needed replenishing. A loud meow from inside the shop drew her attention from the row of sugar jars.

"Barnaby, I hope you haven't done anything I'll have to explain to Mrs Puw tomorrow!" She said, peeking through the curtain. "Barnaby?" She could hear him. But the ginger cat was nowhere to be seen.

"Barnaby Cat, where are you?" She said firmly, stepping into the centre of the shop before listening intently to the room. A pitiful yowl sent Daisy scuttling to her knees and under the large table in the window where a board had come loose.

"Barnaby, are you okay?" Turning on the torch of her mobile phone, Daisy shone it through the hole and peered inside. "There you are!" Barnaby, his eyes big and dark, had squeezed his way inside the frame below the bay window and had twisted around the wooden supports. "What on earth made you decide to go in there?"

Pulling off her oversized cardigan and laying on her stomach, Daisy reached inside as far as she could manage. She could just feel warm fur and wiggled closer to the wall, trying to get a grip on any part of the cat she could find without hurting him. Instead of fur, her fingers found something cold and hard.

"Owww. Barnaby, I'm trying to help you!" In his scared state, Barnaby had swotted her with his sharp claws then wiggled further away and out of her reach.

"What on earth am I going to do now? Daft cat." She said, getting to her feet and moving the table and chairs away from the window and into the centre of the room. Her hand smarted, and she blew on the scratches across her knuckles.

She dialled Tom's number

"Hi. This is Tom—"

"Tom?"

"Leave a message; if this is a police emergency, for God's sake call 999, yeah?" Daisy sighed, her shoulders sagging. She wasn't sure what she'd been expecting Tom to tell her to do, so it was all on her.

The banging on the window made her jump, and her phone clattered to the table. Outside, Sylvia waved at her.

"Daisy!" she mouthed and pointed to the door. "Let me in!"

"Hi Sylvia, bit hectic in here today even though we're closed. Everything alright?" Daisy asked as Sylvia pushed past her.

"Why is your arm black, Daisy? Why are you bleeding?" Sylvia looked around at the shop, which was in a state of disarray. "Is this what you always get up to on your day off?" She tilted her head and squinted her eyes as if she had heard something.

"What's that noise?" Barnaby had obviously had enough of his self imposed entrapment and was growling and hissing.

The windowsill rattled and lifted a little, sending puffs of dust out from the small holes in the wood panelling as he fought to free himself.

"Barnaby decided to go on a mouse hunt, I guess," Daisy said as she pulled at the windowsill. "Can you give me a hand with this? I think we might be able to get in loose."

"Poor kitty." Sylvia said as she pushed up the sleeves of her knitted jumper and grabbed the other end of the length of wood. "If we both hold under the front and pull up, we might be able to free it." Barnaby pushed and the two women pulled, Daisy gritting her teeth as a pain shot through her stiff hip, and with less effort than expected the whole sill pulled off to reveal a very dusty and extremely angry cat.

Not waiting to show any appreciation for his freedom, Barnaby slipped between them with a growl and escaped through the kitchen, leaving only the fluttering of the curtain and a trail of dusty footprints in his wake.

"You're welcome!" Daisy called after him and went to place the sill back in place.

"Wait, Daisy, what's that in there?" Sylvia reached down between the wall panel and the outer stone wall and pulled out a folder and a large leather-bound book. "What a strange place to hide these. What do you think they are?"

"Probably something accidentally left in there by a builder, right?" Daisy said as she peered into the hole as something shiny glinted in the daylight.

Shuddering at the thought of putting her hand down through the thick tangle of cobwebs, black with coal dust and original black mortar, Daisy once again lay down on the floor and reached inside Barnaby's hole. She grimaced as she pushed through the dust and webs, feeling her way along to find the potential treasure.

"To the right a bit." Daisy could feel Sylvia leaning over her and followed her directions. "Little bit more... You got it!"

Daisy gripped the cold, hard object in her fist as Sylvia helped her to her feet and brushed away the worst of the dust.

Opening her fingers, Daisy wasn't quite sure what she was expecting to see, perhaps an old coin or a screw. Instead, she found herself looking at a large gold button that looked like it had come off a wool coat or cardigan.

"I wonder how that got in there. Doesn't even look particularly old considering how clean it is.".

"I don't know, but I guess this is the treasure Barnaby was trying to get at when he got stuck." Unlike the book, which was covered in a thick layer of ingrained dust and cobwebs, the button shone as Daisy held it up between her fingers. A lion's face, nestled in a shaggy mane, stared back at her.

Was this familiar? A vague memory of something shiny tinkling along the floor came and went through her mind and she forgot it as soon as she blinked.

"Mrs Puw is going to go mad when she sees all this mess." Sylvia said with a laugh as she pulled a long dusty cobweb from Daisy's elbow.

"If, not when. Don't worry, I'll make sure everything is clean and tidy before Mrs Puw steps foot in here tomorrow." As Daisy spoke, she emptied the contents of the folder onto the table, spreading everything out. There were books, papers and photographs.

More ancient artefacts to add to her ever-growing collection in her flat?

She turned to the photos, and her heart raced. Each one pictured a much younger Lyle. It took a moment for Daisy to realise that they all seemed to be covert images, taken without his knowledge. There were dates and a circled number on the back.

"Do you know where any of these are taken, Sylvia? I can't seem to place most of them." Sylvia leaned closer, looking over each in turn before patting one with her finger.

"This one is in Carmarthen. I recognise the front of the

bank. I don't think I know the rest of the places, but they all seem to be different banks, don't they? But I do know what this is though." Sylvia had pulled the ledger towards her. "Mammy used to do the Christmas club for the sewing factory. Her ledger looked very similar." She turned to the front of the book.

"This column here is the amount each person named in the first row wants to save over the year. This is the minimum amount they will have to give each week. Hmmm." Sylvia cocked her head to the side as she ran her finger down the last columns.

"Hmm, what?" Daisy asked, leaning over to see what had piqued the young woman's interest. There were more numbers jotted down, this time in red.

"I wonder." Sylvia began flicking back and forth between the front page and each page that had a red mark. "Well, well."

"Sylvia, are you going to tell me what is wrong in this book or am I just going to have to guess?"

"Sorry, my brain has been filled with nothing but baby stuff for so long, it took me a moment to get my head round the numbers."

"And..." Daisy nodded her head slowly in encouragement, trying not to sound frustrated at not understanding what on earth Sylvia was talking about.

"I'd need to look at it with a calculator to make sure, baby brain an' all, but from what I can see, whoever was cooking these books screwed over the savers twice. This number is the total they would have received if they saved this amount each week, right?"

"Right." Daisy glanced over the figures.

"Wrong."

"Wrong?"

"There's only, oh, pennies in it, but this had been going on for years if this is anything to go by. Take this one here, yes? In total, Pamela Gibson was saving £250 over 40 weeks, which should have been £6.25 a week. But this says she needed to pay £6.50. This one here, Mary Wilson, £300 total at £7.50 but told they have to save £8."

"So whoever was in charge of the Christmas savings was pocketing the extra? Wait, you did all that maths in your head?" The realisation awed Daisy, who had no head for numbers and used her calculator for even the simplest of additions.

"I was an accountant in my pre-Freddie life, Daisy." Daisy felt bad for pigeonholing Sylvia with the 'stay-at-home-mother' label and being surprised at her capabilities. "Anyway, that's not all." Sylvia was even more animated now as she waved some papers that she had found in the back of the ledger. "These are the amounts that should be in the bank account each month. Not only was there less than the inflated amount, but there was less than the amount that should have been there. Then suddenly, on this date." She jabbed at the last entry, underlined in red. "Which, if I'm right, is not that long before John Foster disappeared and the account is completely emptied." They both sat staring at each other, trying to put together what they had just read. Had they proved beyond doubt that John had indeed done the terrible things accused of him?

"These are for the business account, and there are withdrawal amounts underlined." Daisy pulled the small pile of bank statements towards them and scanned each withdrawal, noting the number written next to each. "I wonder."

Turning over the photo Sylvia had said was from Carmarthen, Daisy noted the number '6' and scanned through the statements until she found the corresponding number. Underlined was a withdrawal of £3,500 made in Carmarthen.

The date on the back of the photograph and the date on the statement were identical.

Like a logic puzzle that made zero sense until the last vital piece of information was found, everything slotted into place.

"Daisy, you know what this all proves, right?" Sylvia asked, her voice barely above a whisper. Daisy looked back at her and nodded. Lyle had been the one who stole the money all along.

Two women carrying Nordic walking sticks peered at them through the window, paused to look at the closed sign on the door then glancing back to them with confused expressions on their faces.

"Why don't you come on upstairs Sylvia, I'll pop the kettle on. Maybe a cuppa will help some of this make sense." Daisy said, "Sorry, you wanted to tell me about something?"

"I did?" Sylvia paused halfway through collecting the photographs into a neat pile. "Oh yes, you asked about the other night when I was walking Freddie, and I never got round to telling you. I near forgot! It was Ethan that I saw, even though you said you thought he was out of town? Bit of a coincidence with this stuff turning up here, isn't it!" Sylvia stifled a yawn. "A cuppa would be lovely right now. Freddie had me up at the crack of dawn. Peter's in charge of him this morning while I visited a friend. But I got a message when I was halfway there to say her mamgu is poorly, so I was just going to go home."

She saw Ethan?

Daisy ran through everything she knew as they turned towards the kitchen.

"I think you'll find that belongs to me."

Chapter Twenty-One

Daisy jumped at the sound of the voice and gripped onto Sylvia's arm. She laughed when she saw the figure in the doorway. How ironic. Of course it was going to be Ethan. But how long had he been there? Had he heard anything they had just been saying? Maybe she could try to keep him placated. Until what, she wasn't sure.

"Ethan! You made me jump. I didn't know anyone else was here. We're actually closed. Sylvia was just leaving, but you and I can have a cuppa upstairs if you like." As she spoke, Ethan had moved closer, placing himself between them and the front door.

"Daisy." Sylvia's voice was barely above a whisper. Her face had paled, and her eyes were wide with fear.

Daisy plastered on a smile and raised her eyebrows as she tried to send a telepathic message to Sylvia. As if she could read minds, Sylvia let out a nervous laugh and feigned a weak smile.

"I haven't seen you in a long time, Ethan. How are you? Is your mother well?" *Good girl, Sylvia, let's try to keep everything as calm as we can.*

"It was lovely to see you, but I should probably be getting

back home. Freddie will need feeding soon, and Peter will be wondering where I am."

"I'll take those now, please." Ethan pointed to the folder before holding out his hand.

"These? Why would you want these old things? I haven't even had a chance to look at what they are yet. We can look at them together. Upstairs? Let's have that cuppa, yeah?"

Perhaps if they could get past him, they could make a break for it. But Ethan grabbed her, his fingers digging hard into her shoulder. But she refused to drop her smile despite the stabbing pain.

"Daisy, I think you should give them to him." Sylvia pulled Daisy back towards her by her other arm.

"Yes Daisy. Listen to Sylvia, who isn't going anywhere. Give me the books. They belong to me, and I've been looking for them all week." Ethan's voice was grave, raspy, as he tugged the folder out of her grip. He glanced behind them out of the window, but Daisy didn't take her eyes off Ethan's face. His complexion was almost grey, worsened by the big dark circles under his eyes. He seemed to have aged ten years in just a few days.

"Is everything okay, Ethan? You seem distressed. Why don't I make you a nice cup of tea while you look over those books?" Daisy's training kicked in. To offer comfort and support with a calming voice was something she had done many times over the years, both in her job as victim and witness support, but also in the tea shop. Tea always seemed to be the best remedy to make someone feel better. No matter what Ethan may have done, at the core he was still a victim. His father had abandoned him; his stepfather had been a liar and a thief. She reached out to touch his arm with her right hand, trying to ignore Sylvia's shaking hand as it held tightly to her left.

"Get in the kitchen now before someone sees." Ethan snapped away from her as if the touch burnt him and ushered them both through into the kitchen. He pulled the door between the shop and the kitchen closed, something that Poppy had never done, and neither had Daisy. The door refused to pull to, the years of paint making it too big for the frame. Twice Ethan tried to pull it shut, banging the door with anger, before letting out a loud shout of frustration.

Daisy eyed the still open back door. Slowly, she tried to edge Sylvia closer to freedom while Ethan's attention was elsewhere. Small step by small step, the two of them creeping ever closer.

"Don't even think about it." In one long stride, Ethan was once again in their way. In his hand, he held a large knife that he was jabbing towards them. Sylvia let out a small screech and pulled Daisy back towards the corner of the kitchen. Daisy's eyes darted to the knife block on the edge of the work surface. One space lay empty. Without even a second thought, she placed herself fully in front of Sylvia and backed her right into the corner. Sylvia sobbed, her faced buried in Daisy's back.

"Come on now, Ethan, you don't have to do this. Take the book and folder. It's yours; we won't stand in your way, and we'll forget all about this. Right Sylvia?"

"Right. Please, Ethan."

"It's too late now, isn't it! Look what you've made me do?" He waved the knife around. "Nobody is going to believe I wasn't going to hurt you now, are they?"

"We won't tell a soul Ethan, you can go. Nothing has happened; nobody need know anything." Daisy held up her hands, trying to show submission.

"Shut up! Just shut the hell up! I just need a minute to think. You're all the same, aren't you! He just kept on and on too. Didn't give me time to think. Just let me think a minute." Ethan dropped the book onto the island and emptied the contents of the folder. He took a long, slow, deep breath as his finger tapped a fast rhythm on the steel surface. His other hand gripping his hair tightly.

"Right, okay. Here's what's going to happen, yeah? You two just stay there. Be quiet and let me read this and then I'll go, yeah?" Both women nodded silently. "He told me to find this, that I needed to read it to find out the truth. This is what he wanted to show me. That's what I've been trying to find. I thought you had it upstairs in the flat already, but it was just some stupid kid's diaries." As he talked, he leafed through the loose papers, the knife laying forgotten at his side.

"To be honest, I was beginning to think he was lying. That everything I was told about him was true. I'd about given up. You could have knocked me down with a feather when I saw you through the window just now pulling out that old sill. Then, lo and behold, it was just like he said. A book and a folder."

"Your dad told you about those?" Daisy asked. Her voice was calm, quiet.

"Of course it was my dad." He spat back, his hand laying on the knife once more. "He told me what I thought was a tall tale, trying to poison me against my family. He told me he had proof that he'd been run out of town. Tried to get in, didn't we. He had keys an' everything. But after the gate, the keys were the wrong ones." The bang of his fists on the metal reverberated around the room, and Sylvia's fingers dug into Daisy's shoulders. "Stupid man. Why couldn't he just wait?"

Ethan leafed through the book, muttering incoherently under his breath.

"What happened, Ethan? That night?"

"We argued about being locked out. I thought he did it on purpose. But it was an accident. We fought; he fell. The screwdriver just..." His voice caught in his throat, and he wiped away the tears.

"Ethan? What are you doing?" The voice came from the still open back door. Knife in hand, Ethan spun around to face Lyle.

"What are you doing here?"

"I saw you coming this way and wondered what you were doing." Lyle held his hands up defensively. "Put the knife down, son—"

"I am not your son." Ethan screamed, spittle flying from his mouth. He jabbed the knife at Lyle, who stepped back instinctively. "Get over there with them. I need to think a minute." He waved the knife at Lyle, who eased around the edge of the room, hands still in the air. He stood in the opposite corner from Daisy and Sylvia. The back door slammed shut, the movement of air causing the shop door to swing open again and the curtain to flutter.

"Ethan, what did John, your dad, tell you that night?" Daisy tried to keep her voice calm and empathetic, without judgement, like she had been trained to do all those years ago.

"He told me everything, Lyle." Ethan said the name between gritted teeth and looked straight at his stepfather as if he had asked the question.

"Can you tell me, Ethan?" She tried again.

"Why don't you tell them?" He pointed the knife at Lyle as he stepped around the island. "You know what's in these papers? What my dad wrote in this book?"

"No, son—Ethan. I have no idea what that man wrote in there. Whatever it was he told you was all a lie. That's what he did. He lied and cheated and stole. He was a bad man who has twisted you against us, against me, your mother. He ran away like the coward he is, leaving us to deal with the aftermath."

"Stop lying." Ethan screamed with anger, his eyes darkening as he stepped closer to the man who had raised him. "He told me it was you. That you were the one who stole the Christmas savings money and emptied the bank accounts. You befriended him. Wheedled your way into the shop and his trust." He jabbed the knife with each 'you' until the blade was just a few inches away from the older man's chest. "He couldn't tell me why you would do those things, why you seemed to have a vendetta against him. I didn't believe him, of course. Why would you, the man who took care of my mother, who raised me like his own son, have done those terrible, terrible things?"

"That's right, Ethan. You know me; I wouldn't do that. I care for your mother. For you. I sent you to the best school, didn't I? Gave you my home? I was devastated the shop had to close." Lyle held up his shaking hands as he leant back into the corner of the kitchen units.

"But you did, didn't you, old man? You did those things, and I think I know why." The knife pressed into Lyle's jumper, the dent it made in the chunky knit getting deeper. Daisy's mind ran wild trying to think of what had changed his mind. But what could she say? She ran through everything that had happened that week. Then it came to her. The only thing it could be.

"You found the photos of Lyle's grandparents, didn't you, Ethan? When you bro…" she stopped herself, not wanting to aggravate the situation. "When you were in my kitchen. You saw the information I was talking about before, didn't you?" It was working; the knife was barely touching Lyle's chest as Ethan's attention moved to her.

At that moment, a shadow crossed the doorway into the shop. She kept talking, trying not to look as Tom peeked through the curtain. She tried to think fast, but the words came spilling out without thought.

"That's what made you realise your dad was telling the truth, wasn't it? The information about Lyle's family owning the shop with yours?" From the corner of her eye, she could make out Tom holding the curtain apart and stepping in. She flinched as the beads made a chinking noise.

"I saw you that night." Sylvia called loudly from behind Daisy, drawing Ethan's attention back to them. Away from where Tom stood stock still, looking like he was holding his breath. But Ethan's attention and his pale face was back on them. "I saw you heading up the hill. Running away from the shop."

"I knew you must have. I was going to just chuck the screwdriver in the brook and go home to bed, but when I saw you I ran to the park and hid." As he spoke, Tom edged his way closer. He was halfway across the kitchen, and Daisy couldn't believe Ethan still hadn't seen him.

But Ethan was blind to everything but the two women in the corner. Even Lyle, who had been the centre of his attention, was now lost to him.

"I told my mother what happened. She made me wake Hannah and tell her I had booked a surprise trip for us and that we had to leave there and then. Couldn't believe my luck when mam told me about Dafydd. Of course, I still thought my father was the guilty one then, and that you were innocent."

Then everything happened all at once.

As Ethan turned back to Lyle, Tom caught his eye, and he spun round, light glinting off the knife as he gave a surprised shout.

Daisy ran forward to grab Ethan from behind. Her arms tight around his waist fighting against his greater weight to pull him back.

Ethan lunged forward, jabbing the knife in Tom's direction. Tom grabbed the nearest thing to him off the surface and swung a baking tray at the knife but failed to knock it from Ethan's hand.

Taking advantage of Ethan being occupied, Lyle grabbed Sylvia forcing her in front of him like a screaming human shield as he edged around the other side of the kitchen, making a beeline for the kitchen door. He was trying to make a run for it.

Ethan lunged once more, Tom deflecting the blow with his arm, sending the knife clattering to the floor as Daisy grabbed him from behind. With her arms around his body, pulling him into a bear hug, giving Tom the chance to grab his hand twisting it up behind his back.

"Okay now, down on your front, Ethan. Daisy, you can let him go now. I have him." Daisy's thoughts flew back to Sylvia. She spun around, but neither the young woman nor Lyle were anywhere to be seen.

"Sylvia!" she shouted, running to the back door, which was about to slam closed. But before she could get a foot outside, she was greeted with a sight she never expected to see.

There in the back lane, surrounded by an entire team of uniformed officers, were Lyle being handcuffed, Sylvia being comforted by a female officer as she was led from the scene, and DI Locke.

She stepped shakily out into the sun. On the detective inspector's word, the group of officers moved as one into the kitchen.

Chapter Twenty-Two

"Miss Fields, are you hurt?" DI Locke's voice was calm and quiet. She shook her head as she looked back through into the kitchen and saw Tom standing with his hand on Ethan's back, the younger man's face lay flat on the kitchen island as another officer handcuffed him.

It all seemed like a dream. Had Ethan really killed his father? Had he threatened her and Sylvia with a knife? The memory of the light hitting the blade as he jabbed it towards them made her shiver. Had she really grabbed at him? Memories from another day, another knife, a long time ago flashed through her mind. Cold washed over her, and she felt numb to the bone.

"It's his fault. It's not my fault he's dead. It's Lyle's fault. He killed my father." Ethan was shouting sending spittle flying across the surface where she rolled out her biscuits every morning.

"Daisy? Come with me. Let's get you out of the way, shall we? Have a cuppa?" Daisy let herself be led up her steps and into her own little kitchen. DI Locke sat her in a chair and set about making a pot of tea. Her mind was blank; she couldn't think further than the scalding hot cup that was placed in her hands. Locke's voice was a slow monotone drone in the room.

"Come now, drink up. There's plenty of sugar in there." The words brought her back to the room and aware of the heat on her hands.

"Sorry, DI Locke, I don't know what came over me there. Oh, I don't take sugar." She looked down into the deep amber liquid with just a splash of milk, exactly how she liked it.

"Drink it anyway." He said, taking a sip of his own. Dutifully, she did as she was told. The noise at the back door made her jump, and a young police constable in a navy turban appeared in the doorway.

"We have them both in custody, Boss. Miss Wentworth is being taken home by PC Norris, and victim support are going to meet them there."

"Righto Sidhu, take them down to the station and get them checked in. I'll speak with Miss Fields and come down soon to interview them."

"Sure thing Boss." The constable disappeared, closing the door behind him, leaving Daisy alone with the senior officer.

"I know you've had a bad time of it this week, but I'm going to need you to go through everything that happened today. Can you do that?" In contrast with her first meeting with the inspector, this time he was gentle, speaking to her like she were a child. Perhaps because, unlike last time, he had no reason to think she was potentially the killer. Maybe it was because they had the killer arrested and on the way to the station and his job was now mostly getting the confession and filling in paperwork.

Later, Daisy came to think that somewhere deep down, Detective Inspector Locke had come to benefit from his short time in the village, that it had worked its wonders on him. It never occurred to her that perhaps he could see quite how shaken up she was about the whole thing and, as a trained officer, knew he probably should tread lightly to avoid adding to her trauma.

As the hot, sweet liquid slipped down, it radiated through her. The numbness in her mind and body slowly dissipating, and she found herself able to think again. Everything came flooding back to her.

"Why was Lyle arrested? I saw him in handcuffs. You really need to see the paperwork I have downstairs it's all about the… wait. Is Sylvia okay? I don't think she was hurt. My cat. I haven't seen him since just before…Has anyone seen my cat?" Daisy tried to stand, but DI Locke placed his hand on her arm firmly and she moved her chair back under her before taking another sip of her, too sweet for her liking, tea.

"I'll let Sergeant Griffith explain about Lyle. Sylvia is fine, but I'll ask for the doctor to make a house call to check on her, being as that is something they still do here amazingly. I'm not sure what happened to him, but I saw Barnaby chasing a butterfly by the river on my way down here. He seems oblivious to the whole affair. Should I call a vet to see him?" He pulled his phone out of his pocket, his eyebrows raised questioningly, but Daisy shook her head.

He remembered Barnaby's name.

She may not have thought highly of the inspector at first, but remembering an animal's name that to her knowledge he had never been introduced to meant, in her opinion, that he couldn't be a bad person. Could he?

"No, I'm sure he's fine; he just got a bit stuck in the wall this morning…" And so Daisy told the inspector all about everything that had happened, from getting Barnaby freed. To Sylvia working out the ledger, to Ethan holding them at knifepoint, which she refused to admit later had almost brought her to tears to tell it aloud for the first time. Almost. Once she started talking, she didn't stop until she got to the part where she stepped out into the lane.

"So Ethan killed his father! He was so angry with Lyle. I

really do think he could have killed him too today if we hadn't been there."

A thought occurred to her. "It really was Lyle's grandparents that started the shop with John's, wasn't it? I guess something must have happened between them after all."

"After all? What do you mean by that?" DI Locke asked, looking up from his notepad where he'd been writing as quickly as she spoke.

"It's just something from Marianne Pritchard's diaries that I read this morning. About the shops when they were being built. Something about some rumblings between two of the owners. It doesn't specifically say it was at the haberdashers but I bet my bonnet that it was." Daisy reached behind her and took the diary from where she had left in on the sideboard and slid it across the table.

"I'm up to the seventeenth of June. Marianne is hoping her new beau William will ask her to the tea dance on Saturday afternoon. Do you think there might be anything in here that you'll need? I'm really intrigued to find out."

"Not to worry, you keep it. I don't think it will be of any use in this case. Plus, I wouldn't want to leave you on a cliffhanger." The DI slid the book back towards her as he stood "We have all the evidence we need to charge Ethan with the murder of his father, we got a partial fingerprint from the screwdriver and with Miss Wentworth's witness statement I think we'll have him. Although I expect that will be lowered to manslaughter, I really don't think he meant to kill him. Of course, you have to add on the burglary of your flat, as well as today's antics." He shook his head as he walked towards the door.

"We have Lyle arrested for the blackmail of John Foster as well as some other unrelated fraud cases. But from what you've told me, we may also be able to add misappropriation of funds and sheer theft to that list. I'm sure there's something else I'm also forgetting."

He stood silhouetted in the doorway before flicking the kitchen light on to brighten the quickly darkening room. Dark clouds were forming in the sky, threatening imminent rain. Daisy couldn't help but wonder how many women were right that minute running out into their gardens with their laundry baskets shouting for help to gather in their drying clothes before the first droplets fell.

"I will need you to come into the station tomorrow and get this all down in an official capacity, of course."

"Of course, DI Locke. Thank you." He was about to pull the door to when she blurted out, "Before you go, I meant to ask. Why did the police come? How did you know?"

"Well, that's all a bit of happenstance really. Your call to Sergeant Griffith didn't cut off, and it recorded a long but muffled message with 'bleeding' being one of the few audible words. The Sergeant and Constable Grant had at that very moment got some information regarding our Lyle White's family. Turns out their relationship with the Force goes back a very long time. Right back to a certain Mr White, who I expect you'll read all about shortly if your diarist is any good at her job."

"But how did Tom get in? The bell above the door didn't ring?"

"Well... Of course you will be within your rights to put in a claim for the repair. I believe it mostly involved cutting the string while holding the bell to stop it making a noise or falling." Daisy had visions of Tom sneaking through the door with a contraption of scissors and tape.

"My shop. It's not going to open again tomorrow, is it?"

"Afraid not, Miss Fields." The DI glanced down below him and instantly stood straighter, his whole demeanour changing before her eyes. "That's the trouble with crime on the weekend. But we'll be out of your hair as soon as possible, and I'll warn the chaps to tidy up after themselves and not to leave it in chaos like last time." He stepped back and held the door ajar. "Mrs Puw, I am very glad to see you. I'll leave Miss Fields in your capable hands. Bit of a shock, but I made her some sweet tea, and I think she'll survive. Goodbye both."

With a look of suspicion, Mrs Puw, who took her shopping trolley from the young officer who had carried it up the steps for her, gave the inspector a nod, to which he returned with a small raise and stamp of his heels. How strange. Had he done that before? Daisy tried and failed to recall. But before she knew it, she was being fussed and petted over by Mrs Puw who told her all about what had happened, as if she hadn't just lived through it, and insisted Daisy sit by the fire while she made some more tea.

She left the kitchen, taking Marianne's diary with her and leaving Mrs Puw with her hands in the sink doing the washing up and muttering in Welsh to herself. It was all too fast for Daisy, who was still a learner, but she picked out the words terrible man, mess, shop, all punctuated with Daisy's favourite welsh saying "Iesu Mawredd" a frustrated exclamation that literally translates to "Biggest Jesus". Which always tickled her.

As she sat and read, listening to Mrs Puw's clattering of dishes and pans, the delicious scents of a Sunday Roast wafted through the flat, making her stomach rumble. Apart from the toast in bed, she hadn't eaten anything else that day, and it was now midafternoon. Her stomach gave a loud grumble of complaint. As if on cue, Mrs Puw appeared with a plate of sandwiches and fresh tea.

"I thought you might be hungry. I expect you haven't eaten any dinner, and I can bet my last penny that you were not planning on making a Sunday Dinner today, were you? Before all this kerfuffle, I mean."

"It's too much hassle just for me, Mrs Puw," Daisy said, falling on the plate as if she hadn't eaten for a week, not just a few hours. "Mmm, these are lovely, thank you." In quick work, she devoured the cheese and ham sandwiches and sat back in her chair while Mrs Puw nibbled delicately on a single triangle.

"Are you okay, Daisy? I mean, really okay?" Daisy was taken aback by Mrs Puw's sudden concern. Of course, her friend had always shown her love and care, but in her own way, cooking food and fussing was her way of showing affection. But never like this. Never with a worried expression and a quiet tone.

"I'm fine, Mrs Puw, I promise."

"Good. I've invited Tom and Mickey to dinner. Of course, Michael will be here too. I think you should be around people this evening. Not to dwell on what happened." As if overcome by her own manner, Mrs Puw stood quickly and wiped the non-existent crumbs from her housecoat before heading back into the kitchen.

Her hunger satiated and the growing ache in her hip rectified with more painkillers, Daisy curled up to read the diary. Marianne did in fact get invited to the tea dance, and they danced to every single song.

Marianne described William's eyes like pools of deep, cool water. Blue with speckles of white. In the margin she had even tried his surname on for size. Marianne Morgan.

"Mamgu Morgan!" Daisy said aloud. Darlene's name for her own grandmother. This made Daisy laugh, and the last vestiges of cold that had been hanging on inside her were filled with a warmth even the blazing fire couldn't reach.

"Go, Marianne." Daisy said and hugged the old, worn book to her heart.

Chapter Twenty-Three

"Ladies and gentlemen, please don't forget to purchase your locally made tea blends and fresh Welsh cakes before you leave. They have been made on a traditional bake stone while we have been sitting here. You can't get much fresher than that. And if you'd like your own bakestone, Dewi at the ironmongers has some beautiful ones in his window just three doors down!" Mary turned to Daisy with an enormous grin on her face and a sparkle in her eye.

"What?" Daisy asked as she ushered past her with a tray filled with empty cups and teapots.

"Oh, nothing." Mary said, following her into the kitchen and sitting heavily in the old comfy chair.

"No, tell me. Now."

"Well, I've just come from the museum, and there is a huge buzz amongst the staff about a sizeable donation, as well as a new exhibit." She pulled a piece of paper from the tiny pocket of her skirt and held it out to Daisy. It was a memo to all museum staff.

A mandatory meeting is being held between staff and Aubrey and Sons Lock Works on Monday, 12th.

This meeting will discuss the installation of a new exhibit showcasing the long thought lost key and lock design.
Light refreshments provided

"Walter also told me that there will be a meeting with the shop association soon to discuss installing replacement gates and original design keys to those shops who no longer have them. So, there will be a whole aesthetic on the street. All donated by the Aubreys."

"Well, that's great." Daisy said, handing Mary a cup of her favourite Lady Grey. "I'm really pleased the museum is benefitting from this and that the lock manufacturers got their original design back."

"You're pleased?" Mary shook her head. "None of this would have happened if it weren't for you finding those blueprints. That machine was earmarked for scrap because they had nobody who knew how to fix it, or even run it. The factory was on the verge of bankruptcy!"

Daisy felt uncomfortable taking credit for saving a whole factory. But in reality, it was true. The blueprints she had found with Mr Brodbeck's paperwork were the original and only copy to a brand new, yet long lost method of key and lock making. With the factory and enough time, they were able to reapply for the lapsed patent and create an unpickable lock.

"Mary, did you hear that there's going to be a documentary filmed right here?" Michael asked, his arms up to the elbows in soapy water.

"Here in the tea shop? About the killing?"

"No, silly, the village! About the keys! We have one of the few original key and lock sets, though, so I bet they will want to film us here."

"Will you two be quiet about this? I'm really glad the village is getting a nice boost, but I don't want to be dragged into it. I just found some paperwork. Anyone could have done that. Mr Brodbeck should be getting the most praise for keeping his records since the opening of the shop. There's not many businesses that can say that." She sighed before adding, "Plus, I only found it because someone died." Daisy took the now empty tray back out into the tea shop, just as the bell above the door clanged.

It had only taken Tom a few days to fix the bell. But she had missed it while it was gone. She thought about all the times she'd had a headache over the years and had considered removing it violently. But now she gained comfort from the chime and knew she'd never consider removing it again.

"Daisy!" Sylvia, with a frowning, red-cheeked Freddie in a sling on her front, weaved through the tables towards her.

Since what had been termed The Incident happened, Sylvia and Daisy had become firm friends. Even Freddie had developed a soft spot for his new 'Aunty' Daisy, being the type to hand him a biscuit at every opportunity.

On seeing her, his eyes, still watery from crying, brightened, and he smiled a toothy grin as he held out his hand. Daisy glanced at Sylvia, her eyebrows raised questioningly.

"Oh, go on then, you know you spoil this child." Leaving her rapidly filling tray, Daisy headed behind the counter and pulled out a Jammie biscuit. Freddie, on seeing the yummy treat, began to bounce in his carrier and squeal excitedly as only small children in delight can squeal.

"Say ta to Aunty Daisy." Daisy, having no siblings so no chance at nieces and nephews, was still getting used to this valley phenomenon of any close family friends being Aunty and Uncle. Her heart still melted each time she heard it.

"Ta, ta, ta." Jabbered the baby before stuffing the sweet treat into his mouth.

"Are you stopping? Do you want a cuppa? Mary is here" On hearing her name Mary stuck her head through the curtain and waved at Sylvia.

"I shouldn't. I just wanted to show you something. Oh, go

on then." Daisy gestured for the younger woman to go through into the kitchen while she finished clearing the tables. With a quick check that none of the remaining customers needed anything, she followed.

"So what's up?" She asked Sylvia, who had already been supplied with a cup of tea, kept well out of the reach of curious little fingers.

"I've been given a job offer." Sylvia handed Daisy a thin envelope. The letterhead at the top of the enclosed sheets of paper belonged to a law firm in Drehafon.

"I didn't know you were planning on going back to work?" Daisy asked as she flicked through the papers.

"I'm not, at least not until Freddie turns one. But it was always on the cards. I think I'd go stir crazy not using my brain."

"So why did you apply for this?"

"Oh, I didn't! Mr Jones, the senior partner, phoned me a few days ago and asked if he could send me this package. To start whenever I'm ready and home based as much as I like, with a childcare package thrown in too! His firm is dealing with the fallout from the Christmas savings account fraud. They interviewed me to get all the information I knew and how I worked it out. I guess they liked what I had to say and decided they wanted to employ me as a forensic accountant."

"Wow, that's amazing!" Daisy squeezed Sylvia's arm. She knew she had been worried about going back to work, but this seemed just perfect. "And those wages! You're going to say yes, right?"

"Probably! I don't think I can really turn it down. Plus, they are going to pay for whatever training I need, so it'll be back to school for me!" At that moment, Freddie, his face covered in gooey crumbs, let out a big long yawn and rubbed jam into his eyes.

"I think that is my cue to get home," Sylvia said as she stroked his blonde curly hair, encouraging him to lay his head against her chest, despite the jam. "And Daisy. I think there's another tooth coming through, she tapped her own bottom lip to show which one."

"Say no more!" Michael called from the sink where he was towelling dry his arms. "I'll whip up a batch right away and drop them in on my way home." He had become the teething biscuit king, even tweaking Aunty Poppy's recipe for those babies with allergies and adding natural flavours like chamomile and dill to aid with the teething symptoms.

"Well, that's all sorted then. Fingers crossed you won't have to resort to wandering the streets this time."

"Hey, I got a job offer from the last tooth, maybe I'll be offered a new car this time." Sylvia laughed at her own joke before her face fell sombre. "Seems strange to be happy when someone had to die first."

"Try not to think like that or you'll never be happy again." Mary said, standing at Sylvia's side. "Come on, I'll walk you out. I'd best go and check none of my tourists are causing havoc. They seem to think they can barter for anything and everything and caused quite the ruckus at the museum gift shop!"

Sylvia's words echoed Daisy's own feelings. In the two months since The Incident, Aunty Poppy's Tea Shop had been busier than ever. Not just villagers coming to gossip, but more and more people were coming to the village itself. Many of these visitors were true crime fanatics who had listened to a podcast called Killers Cymraeg. The latest series was apparently based on the awaited trial of Ethan Foster. Daisy hadn't been able to bring herself to listen to the podcast, but the chatter around the village was that the Cardiff based pair were going to visit the village to get interviews from those involved and other local people.

Many newcomers were also coming to see the museum, whose name had appeared in newspaper articles regarding both the murder and the lock factory. It was now a daily occurrence that Daisy would find a man, and it was usually men of a certain age, bent down and staring at her gate lock. At first, Mrs Puw had thought they were being odd and shooed them away with a tea towel. But it soon became apparent that this was not going to stop anytime soon, so she gave up.

The final group of newcomers were Daisy's favourite. They were the ones who had seen the museum, or pictures of Commercial Street in the articles about the murder and decided that it looked a lovely day out "despite the obvious."

Daisy wiped down the last table vacated by Mary's tour group just as the bell jangled above the door. Two men, who to Daisy looked like they were probably father and son, looked around them as if wondering if they should wait to be seated.

"Sit anywhere you like," Daisy called over. "I'll just pop these away and I'll be out to take your order. Menus are on the table; today's special bakes are up on the blackboard." She reappeared a few moments later to find them standing at the counter. Daisy, wondering if they hadn't heard. The eldest was pushing eighty if he were a day, and his son was at least sixty.

"Hello there, please do take a seat. We offer table service here."

"Are you Miss Daisy Fields?" The older gentleman asked, and for the first time, Daisy realised they were both wearing business suits and were carrying briefcases. A horrible feeling grew in the pit of her stomach. Was she in trouble? Again?

"Yes? Can I help you, gentlemen?" She said, trying to hide the note of suspicion in her voice.

"As a matter of fact you already did!" Smiles spread across both men's faces and the youngest held out his hand "I'm Theodore Aubrey, you can call me Teddy, and this is my father," She shook his hand before the older man snatched it from his son and squeezed it before pulling her into a bear hug.

"You can call me Ted, my girl. I have been wanting to come and see you for weeks." He patted her back, each one leaving a stinging handprint on Daisy's skin, pulled her away from him and kissed her on each cheek before saying, "Oh come here," and pulled her in for another hug.

"Dad, put the poor woman down, will you? She doesn't know us from Adam, and you're squeezing the living daylights out of her. I'm so sorry, Miss Fields," Teddy said while disentangling her from his father's grasp.

"Oh, it's quite alright. Nothing like a nice big cwtch to make one's day. And please call me Daisy." she said, feeling decidedly windswept. "Why don't I make a nice big pot of tea and we can chat? The sofas in the corner are quite comfortable, and I made sure all the biscuit crumbs were hoovered up from this morning's toddlers. Go and get comfy, and I'll be right over. English breakfast okay, or are you in the mood for something a bit more fanciful?"

"I think we'd best stick to the English Breakfast; my father has had enough excitement for one day. I'm not sure how much more his heart will take." Teddy said, letting his father lead the way across the room.

In the kitchen, Michael, who had obviously been listening at the door, was already setting a tray with three cups.

"Sure does like a cwtch, that one, doesn't he? Let me just…" He grinned as he reached out and flattened down her hair, which had been left at a jaunty angle from the elder Aubrey's embrace.

"What do you think they want?" She asked, opening a tub and plating up some shortbread cookies, the edges of the side plate covered in delicate wildflowers.

"Why are you worried, silly? I don't think they want anything more than to see the person who helped save their factory and thank them in person!" Michael handed her the tray, turned her around and led her back into the tea shop with a shove.

Chapter Twenty-Four

From her seat at the top of her steps, Daisy enjoyed the last vestiges of golden sunlight before it crept below the mountaintops. As a child, she had imagined that the mountains were like a big bed and the sun was tucking itself in for the night. She loved this time of day and sat in this very spot at sunset as often as the weather allowed. Which, given the fact that Wales has a tendency to be wet and cloudy, is not as often as Daisy would like.

Barnaby, who had been a decidedly more spoilt cat since The Incident, trotted his way across the lane carrying an acorn in his mouth. Dropping his gift on the step next to her, he nuzzled it towards her hand before stretching out across her feet.

"Well, thank you, my Barnababyboo. You are a good boy. Yes, you are" She rubbed his belly, relishing the loud purrs emanating from his chest and the soft warm paws that held her hand to him.

"That cat has got you wrapped around his little finger, you know." Daisy jumped at Tom's voice. He appeared at the bottom of the steps, a zipped up hoody pulled over his uniform.

"Cats don't have fingers." She rolled her eyes as she poured him a mug of tea whilst dying inside at the thought he had hear her say Barnababyboo. She hoped the diminishing light hid the redness that flushed her face and chest.

Out of habit, Tom stuck his nose in the mug and gave a quizzical expression before taking a sip. Today, Daisy had opted for a milk oolong tea. Tom grabbed a teaspoon and added two heaped spoonfuls of sugar before taking another drink.

"I don't know why you can't just drink normal tea like everyone else."

"I'm pretty sure the sales ledger of my little tea shop disputes your 'everyone' comment there." Daisy said, nudging him with her foot, eliciting a small mew from Barnaby.

As they drank, they sat in silence watching the bats swooping over the field opposite. Daisy always set out an extra mug for Tom on these evenings when he wasn't working late. He usually appeared like magic before the pot was empty. Some days they sat for hours talking about their days, the past, the future and anything wrong with the world that needed to be set right. On other days, they sat in companionable silence watching the changing of the day to night. This evening seemed to be one of the latter days. There was never any awkwardness between them. They had been friends for far too long for that.

"Talking about ledgers." Tom broke the silence after a long five minutes of watching a frog bounce out from the long grass, into the lane. The frog seemed surprised at the situation and wandered in a large circle before disappearing again through the fence and down into the river beyond.

Ledgers? Daisy thought, scrapping her memories of their previous conversation and deciding his comment was a stretch at best.

"We heard from the CPS this morning. They are going ahead with an involuntary manslaughter prosecution. If Ethan pleads guilty, he could be lucky enough not to serve too much time, and that would only be because of the attempted assault and kidnap of you and Sylvia. Obviously, I can't go into detail. But reading his statement about that night with his dad, I think it was all just a horrible accident." Tom fell into silence again.

"And Lyle?" Daisy asked, wondering if she was pushing her luck to get some more information.

"Oh, Lyle." Tom laughed and shook his head. "That one will take so much time to explain we'd need another pot of tea!"

"I'm sure I can manage that. Come on in while I boil the kettle." Grabbing the tray, Tom followed her inside, and she listened to his excited chatter as the kettle bubbled to life.

"Poor Moira opened up to one of our victim support staff." He said, dipping his hand into the biscuit tin, "Once he moved in, it seems he was keeping her practically locked up in her own home. As soon as she found out he'd been arrested though, she started talking and didn't stop. Told us everything! The fraud investigation alone is huge. But it seems he had been planning his attack on the shop for years. He was told all his life that his grandparents were pushed out of the shop by the Fosters, and he wanted revenge for his family's legacy being stolen out from under him."

"Well, I don't know if this can be of any official use to you. But I have something you need to read." Daisy headed into her bedroom, coming back with not only one of Marianne's diaries but also two crocheted blankets.

"No, I think I'll live." Tom said, looking at the pale blue one she held out to him.

"Don't win any prizes for being cold, you know. Even big, tough men get chilly." Daisy replied, following him back outside and sitting on the top step before throwing her favourite shawl, old and fuzzy in a lovely cream, around her shoulders and then around her legs as she tucked her knees up to her chest. She flipped through the darkened, yellowed pages, pausing occasionally until she reached the passage that she wanted.

"How about I read it to you?" She said, peering at Tom over the top of the book. The biscuit tin had found its way outside on the tray, and he had his thumb in his mouth sucking the chocolate from a dipped Viennese finger. He just shrugged and grabbed another.

"Remember, she was running the small cafeteria for the builders? Well, at this point in the diaries, she's married to William Morgan, living in Elizabeth Way and is working in the mine cafeteria instead. No children yet" Daisy only had a few of the diaries left to read and had slowed down as she didn't want the saga to end. She had cried for hours reading about the aftermath of a mine shaft collapse. Her heart broke for the families, some of whom had descendants still living in the village today.

She had blushed and flicked quickly through a few pages of their honeymoon, feeling like she was intruding on Marianne's privacy.

"Wednesday, November 3$^{rd.}$ 1891," Daisy read aloud.

"Today, there was such a ruckus in the village. Mr Young and Mr Foster were brawling in the middle of the street! The ash men's horses were spooked and almost bolted up the road. Rumour has it that Mr Foster had caught Mr Young out in a fib and confronted him about it. Mr Young became defensive.

"Sergeant Knockes was called, and they were both marched to the station. Mrs Young and Mrs Foster were so shamed, they hid inside the shop and refused to come out. Luckily, today is a Wednesday, so the shops are all closed half day, as I expect they would have been overrun with women suddenly in need of buttons or pins who were just looking for idle talk to fill their boring lives.

"Willy says that Mr Foster was in The Farmers Arms tonight, but the police were still holding Mr Young. It turns out he has been pilfering from the till."

Daisy flicked forward through the pages. "Then the next we hear of them is..."

"Friday, November 5$^{th.}$ 1891

"Mr Young was collected by the constabulary today. Sergeant Knockes had no idea they were coming until the Black Maria turned up at the station first thing. The carriage sent a chill through me as it past me outside the bakers. It was like a large black coffin, no windows and only bars on the door, and it shone! Even on a grey day like today, the black paint was dazzling.

A crowd gathered at the station while they arranged for Mr Young to be brought out. I thought our Sergeant Knockes and the other officers at the station were smart in their blue uniforms with their caps. But these officers stood burly and tall in their long wool coats, the gold adornments on their round helmets gleaming.

And they were all so rough and sullen. Of course the sombre situation warranted a sense of seriousness, but one of Jones the Butcher's youngest boys was clipped around the ear by one of them just because he wanted to see them up close. The poor boy went crying away to his mother clutching the side of his face. Mrs Jones said later that he left a bruise in the shape of the constable's ring!

Eleanor is such a lovely woman I truly feel for her being married to that brute. I know for a fact that he beats her, saw him rip her blouse in the gulley behind the church just a fortnight ago. I wonder if this will be the last we see of him, and her and their boys will be free."

Daisy turned to the back of the book

"Saturday, December 25th, 1891

What a joyful Christmas Day it has been. Mammy and Aunty Blodwen made a wonderful dinner between their two ranges. Uncle Jack raised the geese. Willy grew the potatoes, carrots and himself, and they have been stored in the loft along with the apples and pears Mrs Del let us pick from her orchard this harvest. I was charged with boiling the plum pudding and baking the mince pies."

Tom raised his eyebrows at her.

"I'm getting to it. I just found this so lovely I wanted to share" She shook her head, but skimmed past the remaining whimsy of Christmas past until she got to the relevant part.

"After church this morning, I saw Eleanor crying and hugging Mr and Mrs Foster. We tried not to earwig, but it was difficult not to. She was thanking them profusely and hugging them all over again. Mr Young is spending at least the next year in prison, and she had begged Mr Foster if they could buy out her share of the shop as she wanted to travel back to her hometown with her boys. I guess this morning he had given her the money and the forms all signed showing that she was released from any business related responsibility.

"Aunty Melly lives next door to her, and she said she was packing the boys into the back of the milk cart and Dai the Milk was taking her to meet the train this very afternoon."

Closing the book, she sighed and took a sip of her tea. She noticed that Tom had pulled the blanket over his knees but didn't dare comment on it. The clouds in the sky were shades of purple, grey and dark reds and a sudden chill was in the air.

"So there was no stealing of the shop, and the Fosters had actually helped the family out of debt by buying them out of their share." She said, leaning against the wall.

"He was arrested in our station." Tom was getting to his feet as he spoke and took the steps down two at a time.

"Where are you going?"

"Lyle has been trying to claim that the shop was stolen from the family. If Mr Foster used a solicitor to help get him released from this fight, as well as the theft, they would be the same ones who helped sort the dissolving of the business."

"Okay, but how does knowing that help? And...I don't understand."

"Because we'll still have the paperwork at the station. If we have the name of the solicitor, hopefully they will have evidence that the business was sold legitimately. He's trying to claim that the familial distress caused him to act the way he has, and this means he won't have a leg to stand on." He bounded back up the steps, grabbed the book from her lap and rubbed the top of her head, sending her hair flying in various directions. "Well done, Daisy Chain. You're good at this detective stuff even when you're not trying."

"Don't call me Daisy Chain." She said to the mountains opposite. Tom's heavy footsteps already echoed through the arch and out onto the street behind the shop.

Epilogue

Moira stood in the doorway, her bottle green apron matching the fresh paint of the shop front. She smiled out at the gathered crowd, held up her hand and cleared her throat. Daisy felt a tingle of pride run through her as the chatter reduced to a buzz of excitement and all eyes turned to face the woman who once tipped her teacup from nerves.

"Hannah and I would like to thank you all for the support you have shown us in recent months. Not just in the opening of our little venture here, but in our personal lives as well." A ripple of hushed comments ran through the crowd.

"If anyone had told me a year ago that not only would my daughter-in-law and I would be opening our very own shop, but that my husband John—" Her voice cracked and her hand reached up to her throat "That John's name would be cleared of any wrongdoing even if...Well, anyway." She took a deep breath as Daisy held her own, only letting out a long slow sigh as Moira pushed on. "Today, Hannah and I would like to welcome you to the grand opening of Foster's Fabric Crafts. A place to not only purchase all your crafting necessities. But somewhere to learn, from cross stitch to embroidery, how to replace a lost button, or let down a hem in your children's school trousers, anyone is welcome to come to us for help. Please come on in. There are activities to try and some light refreshments care of Poppy's Teashop."

She stood aside to a round of applause as people swarmed through the door, each one hugging her or shaking her hand as they passed. Daisy slowly made her way forward at the back of the queue, wanting to catch Moira without holding anyone else up.

"Moira, this place looks amazing! You've both worked so hard, and you deserve the best of luck." She kissed Moira on the cheek and held her at arm's length to look at the front of her apron. Embroidered across the top was the name of the shop, in gold thread to match the hand-painted sign above the window.

"Do you like it?" Moira fingered the neat swirl of the lettering. "Hannah embroidered them as a surprise! She's so clever." She peered inside at her daughter-in-law with a wistful smile on her face. Hannah, wearing a matching apron, was surrounded by a small crowd and seemed to be answering questions about her embroideries that hung on the walls.

Inside, the shop was bright and welcoming. There was colour everywhere. A large rainbow shaped display of button tubes welcomed you inside, each topped with a single button to show the contents. Daisy found it hard to believe there was such a variety of buttons to be had.

There were shelves filled with fabrics and baskets labelled with everything a good haberdasher would stock, from knicker elastic to packets of pins. Among the essentials, there were beautiful items for sale, from large hand sewn pictures to tiny decorations.

A long white table took up the centre of the shop. Every chair was filled with someone trying out a small craft project. Daisy could see children attempting oversized cross stitch and even Bobby and Iestyn, the two teenagers who had carried

Darlene's boxes up to the flat, were laughing as they each wrapped wool around card to make sparkly pink pompoms.

"How is Hannah doing now?" Daisy asked, keeping her voice low enough for others not to hear. Moira guided her away from the door.

In the months since The Incident, Moira had become a new woman. She was seen around the village daily, had started attending chapel and the Ladies Guild weekly meetings again, as well as volunteering with Llun Lles and at the community centre. Daisy had watched her blossom from the cowering shell of herself into the smiling woman who walked with a spring in her step, smiling and greeting everyone she met. But Hannah had become quiet and withdrawn.

"Ethan is still waiting for his court date, but he was so badly affected by what he did. His own dad, I mean.. that they've moved him to a secure psychiatric unit. Mr Eisenberg is confident that he'll serve minimal time because of the extenuating circumstances, with Lyle and everything. Hannah's doing a bit better now he's in the unit and is getting proper help. I've even managed to get her to see the doctor to start looking after herself too. The shop really brought her on. Something for us both to work at and get out of our own heads a bit."

"That's really good. She looks so much better. I heard Lyle is still trying to claim the shop was stolen from the family, even with the evidence they found at the station?"

"There is so much more than that now. John had been doing his homework, and the stuff you found in the shop was just the tip of the iceberg. John had been gathering evidence about Lyle for years. He had a whole portfolio that was sent to the police after he died. He also instructed his solicitor to deliver a parcel to me. Apparently, Lyle knew about a... let's say a minor indiscretion that had happened on a drunken night in the city. John was mortified it had ever happened and wanted to tell me. But then he found out about the stolen money and confronted Lyle. I don't know what was said between them, but Lyle twisted it so much that John believed he would be blamed for it all and leaving was the only way to save his reputation and the shop."

"I don't think I understand?" Daisy frowned, then smiled and waved to Sylvia through the window, where she was showing Freddie a small hand sewn dog.

"Daisy, I don't even begin to understand myself. I think the stupid man thought that if he left, he could prove he was innocent. But then the whole thing blew up in his face. The valley thought he was the one who had stolen all the money, and by that point he was too afraid to come back. If he'd just stayed and been honest with me, we could have worked it out. But it was just like him to make a rash decision." Moira shook her head and sighed a long, deep, frustrated sigh.

"So what was in the parcel he sent you?"

"There were lots of old letters and cards for either me or Ethan, that he'd written and either chickened out of sending altogether, or had been returned to sender. You can guess whose handwriting was on those envelopes! And there was a copy of his will." She reached into the pocket of her apron and pulled out a well-thumbed letter and handed it to Daisy, who scanned through the pages.

"He left you everything?" She asked as she finished reading. From what she could see, John had owned commercial properties in lots of small towns, as well as the flat where he'd lived in Cardiff Bay. She didn't like to read too much into the numbers, but Moira would never need to worry about money again.

"Including this shop." Moira ran her hand down the shiny green paint of the window frame, her eyes landing on the photographs hung inside that Daisy hadn't noticed earlier. There were photos of John's family, dating right back to the first Fosters. In pride of place was a photo of John, large tailoring scissors in hand and laughing as he looked over the cutting table at the person behind the camera. "When I realised we had the property and the money, I thought it would do us both the world of good. Hannah has always been so good with a needle and thread. I always thought it was a shame the haberdashers had gone because it would have been perfect for her."

As if on cue, there was a rapping on the window that made them both jump and laugh. Hannah, with wide eyes, was beckoning them inside. She looked excited but totally overwhelmed.

"You should go in and rescue her, poor girl. I'll follow you in," Daisy said with a laugh as Hannah disappeared into the crowd again. Moira made her way to the door, but stopped to look back at Daisy.

"I don't know if I ever thanked you." Moira said with a sombre note in her voice.

"You don't need to at all. I didn't really do anything."

"You coming to the house that day, everything you said and did. You really helped me see what was happening and try to be brave. I don't think we'd be in this position if you hadn't. So thank you." She disappeared inside the shop leaving Daisy stood outside watching the futures of two hurt women coming life before her eyes.

A little extra just for you

Would you like to read the full Christmas Day entry from Marianne Morgan's 1891 diary?

Head over to https://BookHip.com/ZGFJHHW to download your copy.

Cymraeg - English Dictionary

Duw Duw - Literal translation "god god" form of exclamation
Nefi blw - "navy blue" - probably taken form "nefoedd/heavens" but altered to an interjection that avoids offending others.
Iesu Mawr/mawredd - Big jesus. Good God/Jesus Christ. An expression of surprise
O dammo'r ymenydd - my damned brain – forgotten
Bach - Small, meaning little one
Dim ots cariad - No worries love
Cariad - Love
Bore da - Good morning
Edrych - Look
Bachgen da - Good boy
Bechgyn dda - good boys
Nawr te - Now then
Hisht nawr - quiet now
Cwtch - A special welsh cuddle, meaning a small, safe place. Also used for the cupboard under the stairs
Mamgu - Grandmother

Not Welsh language, more welshisms
Gulley - small lane, walkway between streets/houses
Now in a minute - An undetermined amount of time that will possibly be soon

If you find any more that I've missed from this list feel free to get in touch via my social media pages or by emailing me on
katie@katieoneilmysteries.com

About the Author

Katie O'Neil was born and raised in the South Wales Valleys. A mother of five, Katie lives with her husband, the two youngest children and the two family dogs, Stanley, the tiny Poochon and Bee, the huge Irish Wolfhound. Katie has always loved reading and visited the local library multiple times a week as a child and teen, always trudging up the hill to home with the maximum amount of books allowed.

Katie's love of reading never waned and writing was a natural progression. Her first books were tiny ones, written as a small child for her Sylvanian Families and held together by a single staple. Having penned many things from terrible poems full of teenage angst to a popular (but now defunct) blog, Katie decided to give books another try. This time real ones, with no staples in sight...unless she can work it into a murder weapon somewhere.

Printed in Dunstable, United Kingdom